SUNSET

by

Judith Petres Balogh

USA ▪ Canada ▪ UK ▪ Ireland

Note for Librarians: A cataloguing record for this book is available from Library and Archives Canada at www.collectionscanada.ca/amicus/index–e.html
ISBN 1-4120–9148–9

Printed in Victoria, BC, Canada. Printed on paper with minimum 30% recycled fibre. Trafford's print shop runs on "green energy" from solar, wind and other environmentally–friendly power sources.

Offices in Canada, USA, Ireland and UK

Book sales for North America and international:
Trafford Publishing, 6E–2333 Government St.,
Victoria, BC V8T 4P4 CANADA
phone 250 383 6864 (toll-free 1 888 232 4444)
fax 250 383 6804; email to orders@trafford.com
Book sales in Europe:
Trafford Publishing (UK) Limited, 9 Park End Street, 2nd Floor
Oxford, UK OX1 1HH UNITED KINGDOM
phone 44 (0)1865 722 113 (local rate 0845 230 9601)
facsimile 44 (0)1865 722 868; info.uk@trafford.com
Order online at:
trafford.com/06–0902

10 9 8 7 6 5 4 3 2

To my two daughters, my best friends:
Christina Cantrell and Andrea Majorczyk.

Their understanding, unconditional love, and unfailing support are the gifts in my life. I am especially grateful for their seemingly endless reserve of humor, never–failing good cheer, and positive attitude.

In order to avoid incorrect and useless guessing: this is not a story of either of them. The characters, dialogs, situations and locations are purely fictional, and have nothing to do with these two excellent women. The story does not depict anyone, or anything in real life.

I would also like to express special thanks to Dr. Aniko Tanko (Mrs. L. Karvalits) for her input on medical questions; to Clyde E. Atkisson, Alberta Brown, Bill Hobbs and JoAnn Johnson (DoDDS educators) for their kindness and relentless help; to Dr. Andrew L. Stangel for opening to me the world of art; to authors Nuala O'Faolain and Douglas Arvidson for giving me hope when so many things failed; and last but not least to Susan Szappanos, Maria Friedrich, and Rose Pohly for promoting my books, especially at the breathtakingly beautiful Hungarian Heritage Museum in Cleveland.

"Most often your earthly creation will be evaluated not by you,
but how other individuals will receive it. "

Clyde E. Atkisson, jr. in his book: <u>Be, Create and Change</u>

⊛ Sunset

ONE

Katharina just returned home after taking care of several irritating errands in town, and immediately shed her confining street clothes and heels. Having made herself comfortable in robe and slippers, she brewed a cup of tea, which was her idea of a pacifier. Thus regaining her equilibrium after the compounded annoyances of the afternoon, she turned on the computer, and found her daughter's note waiting for her.

"Mom, I really feel your pain about your loneliness; I would be a world class monster if I didn't. But then as soon as I almost reach the point of absolute empathy, strange thoughts emerge from the warehouse of my erratic and perhaps wicked subconscious. I then begin to fantasize about living alone, like you do now, and I find it appeals to me at a certain level, because this living alone business does have charms, although certainly unmentionable in polite company.

Don't get me wrong. I love my family dearly and never, not for a split second, would I want to be without them. But you do remember, don't you, the games we used to play when I was small? You would ask the question 'What if…' and I would have to come up with some answers, which at least in the beginning, were mostly silly, off–the–wall– responses in the manner of small children, who have not thought about the topic before. You'd ask what if we could fly, what if the streets were all water like rivers flowing right at our door, what if we could read each other's thoughts, and so on. In the beginning I would give predictable answers, appropriate for my current age group, such as 'It would be fun', or 'I'd go crazy'. But you never accepted such responses and prodded me with more questions, until we thoroughly discussed the issue while we had great fun. You led me to think in a more focused way, and I am convinced that my success in business life is due to these games. You taught me to think 'out of the box'.

So I now play a 'what if' game, like we used to do in the old days. The question and the responses to it are purely fantasy, nothing to do with real life. But like so often lately, I get tired easily, see the world all draped in black, and have a great desire to downsize the architecture of my complicated life. Not really, not actually, but at times I do wish to escape, if only for a momentary interlude. You do know how a fish comes up to the surface for a breath of air before it sinks back into the depths again to go after its domestic business, such as what to fix for dinner. That is what I need. Have you ever tried on an outrageous dress in a store, although you had absolutely no intention to buy it? I have. Just for the heck of it. In this spirit I want to play the game of "trying on". I am not buying, mind you, just visiting the fitting room for fun. So here it goes: what does it feel to be alone, like you are now?

With no laundry from two grownup daughters. With no knee–high shit in the basement. A garage where I can actually put my car, because it has no tools and sport equipment in it. French toast for dinner, if I don't want to cook. Anyhow, who ordered a woman to have a seven–day, 52 week workload without a single day off, all to be done after she comes home from her paying job? By the way, do you know what the great compensation for labor pains is? We can stay off our feet for a few days, and get breakfast in bed! Those are mighty powerful perks, if you ask me. Some women I know might prefer to stay in the hospital until the kid is off to college. I have a friend who has terrific connections and is a gifted actress when she needs to be. She finagled for herself a gallbladder operation. Same reason. She loved the hospital stay, which was all too short. Later she practiced Wicca on those men, who decreed that short stays at the hospital are beneficial. For whom? As far as that goes, I could aggressively demonstrate against the curtailing of this basic human right. Cut down the length of maternity stay in the hospital, and watch the population dwindle.

And Gary gets crabbier and crabbier. He just bitches about everything. And he denies that he is bitching. The girls call him Groucho. To his face. And he thinks they are kidding. They are not.

I am tired of being the maid. I am tired of coming down in the morning to pick up all the cups and crumbs from the coffee table. I am tired of coming home from work to find the dishes on the table from the breakfast they made after I left for work. I never know what to cook, and the laundry multiplies like rabbits in a year of plenty and no natural enemies. I'm tired of Gary's mother. Really tired.

I do not want anything that needs to be fed or taken for a walk or cleaned up. No dogs, especially not the kind that loves to argue with skunks. No fish. Nothing that does not belong to me. I am tired of power tools in my kitchen, next to paperclips, loose change, old stubs, three used batteries, a wristwatch, which stopped running when Karen graduated from kindergarten, also matches, washers, keys that no longer open anything, can openers of various shapes bearing names of forgotten vacation spots, rubber bands in the melting stage, and a long list of other objects having no use whatsoever. Mind, these things don't belong to me; they are neither my possessions nor are they next of kin. These should not be living on my countertop next to the breadbox.

I am tired of Karen's furniture in my basement. I am tired of her pain, which I cannot solve any more than she can. I am tired of shoes. They all hurt. I am tired of the dog farting all the time, because they feed her chocolates. I am also tired of being the only one who walks and feeds the same damned dog. Except for chocolate and potato chips. They do feed her that at the wag of a tail. I want to live on a beach and walk barefoot all day. Without his mother."

Katharina stopped reading her daughter's e–mail, and walked to the window with her cup of tea. While she suffered from lethal inertia, the garden continued to be lush and well tended, thanks to the gifted gardener Martin found some years ago. Mr. Klausen loved his work passionately and considered the garden to be his very own territory, where he could express all his dreams without any interference. He appeared regularly with his tools and flats of plants, and unless Martin or Katharina had a special request, he worked the acre–and–half with impeccable taste, and according to his own ideas, turning the garden into a source of constant pleasure. At this season he arranged great clusters of white, purple and yellow chrysanthemums to appear like small hills, so bright that even on bleak days they gave the impression of hidden sunshine. The pond was now completely covered with water–lilies, appropriately called in some languages fairy–roses, frustrating the purpose of the scantily clad marble lady, whose job was to fill her jug with water; a very difficult task on account of the fairy flowers. Mr. Klausen, a judicious gardener, kept the imperialistic purposes of the water lilies under control all summer, but toward the end of the season he let them luxuriate and expand as much as they wanted; of course they wanted almost the entire pond. She gazed out at the lovely garden, and thanked Providence that this world also houses artists, who can make the dreams of others come true.

Her thoughts returned to the e–mail message. She laughed, when she read the note; Alexa always sent outrageous messages, because she knew well enough that they made her mother laugh. She was a fanatic believer in the healing power of laughter, and she also knew that her mother was in great need of that. Alexa believed that if Fate knocked you down, the only way to survive it is to get up and laugh into its face, because laughter has the power to chase away those ill winds, which inevitably bring destruction, self–pity, depression, disorientation and all the related miseries mankind uses to make things even worse. If she had no time to write a note, she at least forwarded some choice jokes. She saw to it that her mother had a daily dosage of merriment.

As always, Katharina enjoyed her daughter's rambling, inconsequential discourse. As expected, her spirit did lift, and as a result the brainless bureau-cracy, which had unnerved her earlier, stopped being irritating. But as she watched the moving clouds from her window, a disquieting heaviness settled over her. Where is the end of humor and of lightheartedness, and where does trouble begin? It was certainly hard to tell with her only daughter. How much of her bravado is her true self and how much of it is merely a well–rehearsed role–play for the benefit of those whom she does not wish to disappoint with her easily hurt soul, or share the troubles she faces daily? A mother, according to popular belief, should always know, but Katharina was clueless. She liked to think that she understood her daughter. She knew her face, her moods, her functions and dysfunctions, but in the end, she knew that there existed an invisible wall, which closed her out from those carefully guarded innermost chambers. Katharina more or less accepted this, because there were so many other compensations in their relationship with each other, but at times, when worry about Alexa overwhelmed her, she wished that she knew more about her daughter's inner life.

With the passing of years, most people, excluding only the pathological gossips, are increasingly more reserved. Alexandra, like the rest of mankind, was unknowable, or at best only partially open, because mortals decide at one level of their consciousness how much and how accurately they would reveal themselves to others. Even mothers only get a reflection of their grown children's inner life. She continued to gaze at the garden.

For Katharina the evening hours, when the world shows its most appealing face, have always been the favorite part of the day. Trees and bushes sit at the rim of their elongated shadows, and as day is done peace settles over the manicured garden of the place she called home for ten years. The rush of the day over, the leisure and pleasure of the evening still ahead, the hour was always full of promises. It was filled with expectation as she listened for the sound of his approaching car. His car, now silent in the garage, was probably nursing its own grief. I really ought to sell it, she reflected whenever she saw it, but knew that she could not yet do it.

The house, once filled with flowers and warmth, now felt alien. Her heart was hollow and she stopped caring about a great many things. Alexandra's message, stripped of the light humor, dropped like a heavy stone into the cold and dark depth of her very being, where her passions were numb and rigid, like the earth during the winter freeze. Yet, on its way to nowhere, the barely concealed discontent of her daughter scratched the deadened surfaces of what was once Katharina's soul, and it left a dull ache in its wake. The charm of the afternoon was meaningless since he was gone, and now Alexa's humor–coated message took away what was left of the fragile tranquility.

Autumn did not yet strip the foliage, but painted the trees with a perfect Venetian tint; the air was still mild. Martin and she used to take long walks at this hour, and enjoyed the departing day with all their senses. That was an eternity ago. Before he became ill. Before he lost his strength. Before she learned to smile in the face of disaster and to lie to the man she loved.

Although he had a bad case of influenza with gastrointestinal complications in the fall of the year before, he was well again for the cruise they planned on a glamorous ship at the end of December to celebrate their tenth wedding anniversary and also the beginning of the second millennium. They were invincible and in high spirits. Life was good.

On their return he felt out of sorts, and first shrugged it off. "Too much champagne and lobster. Too many nights staying up dancing. We overestimated ourselves, just because we feel young." At the end, he had to admit that not everything could be blamed on the good life. He went to see his doctor, who sent him to a specialist, who asked for consultations. After surgery they tried chemo, promised cures, or at least remission, urged him to fight for his life, cited patients, who lived a useful life after the diagnosis. Three months later he was dead. This is how fast cancer worked on him.

She did not cry at the funeral, and everybody admired her wonderful strength. They likened her dignified self–control to that of Jacqueline Kennedy's at the President's funeral. But Katharina was not strong at all; she was merely in a state of shock, and did not fully comprehend what was happening around her. Reality struck her much later. To be quite exact, it was on a stormy night in early April. She woke up shivering, because the house felt cold. Gone was the balmy spring weather; a raging wind was howling in the garden, branches, like fleshless fingers scraped at the bedroom window, and the rain came down in sheets. While not actually afraid of storms, at her age that would have been ridiculous, she always craved the closeness of someone during bad weather. Instinctively she moved in the big double bed and stretched her hand toward Martin. "Martin, I'm freezing. Aren't you cold?" she whispered in half sleep. And then it hit her with the brutality of a pneumatic hammer. He was no longer there. He was in his cold grave; rain pounding on the fresh mound. The buried pain, so intense that at first she thought it was physical, burst forth with an elemental force. Martin, I'm so scared, she sobbed. Alive, scared, and so alone. My life is just a shadow of what is has been; my soul is sick. The house and I don't count the days since you have gone. Come back, or take me away; I can't go on without you.

And then she gave up pleading for Martin's return; even she knew that it was futile. She hugged her pillow and said the only prayer she knew that night: please God, show some mercy and give peace to my soul, and help me to survive this loss.

She cried until exhaustion made her fall asleep again, and then for days after it she never even left her bed. She entered a dark tunnel, which appeared to be one–way only. A silent Rosie cleaned dutifully; Alexa came and went, and eventually brought Dr. Ed Collins, who sat with her for a while. He talked about the legitimate grief she felt, and said that it was to be expected and it was part of the healing process. He promised that the fierce pain would lessen in time and that she would find her old self and get well again. She nodded in agreement and did not believe a word of it. He gave her a tranquilizing shot and quietly left the room. And then she slept and hoped never to wake up again.

Six months have passed since, but the pain although no longer the screaming horror of the first weeks, was still very much part of her days, as were those dark episodes, which hit her unexpectedly and with the same intensity she felt in the beginning. When she thought the worst was over, it came back hard again, and again. It did not take much to bring on the grief. A song, a book, some personal item of his, which she found as she wandered in the big house, a piece of mail still addressed to him, a special day, or the empty weekends; anything and nothing could waken the demons. Life then appeared meaningless, all efforts useless and a diffusion of time, emotions, and thoughts turned life into an impenetrable fog, and she moved around enervated, not finding peace, nor purpose any more. At such times she had to force herself to do all the things needed in order to continue with life. If it were not for Alexa's sometimes abrasive humor and unconditional love, she would probably have turned to the wall and given up altogether.

Her thoughts returned to the present. Alexa's message should not be taken seriously, she told herself as she watched a swarm of tomtits land on the feeder in front of the window. They were always hungry, but rather reserved in their habits. Looking left and right with nervous little jerks, watching constantly for real or imagined danger, they hopped ever closer to the feeding station, then waited patiently for their turn. When the air was clear, they dived to the platform and after a last glance around to make certain that cats and similar enemies were not lurking nearby, politely picked up one seed. Only one. They darted away quickly and alighted on a near branch with their bounty, and let their next of kin to the table of plenty. Something people ought to learn, she reflected; no greed, no elbowing, no fighting, but civilized and reserved behavior, like the English queuing up for the trolley.

Alexa could be quite dramatic to be sure, Katharina assured herself as she turned from the window, but most of the time she was brilliantly funny, often in unexpected ways. Her humor was fresh and vibrant, different from Katharina's. This was the only point where the generation gap showed: Alexa could easily and in a hilarious manner say all sorts of shocking things, but Katharina, although she enjoyed her daughter's wit, was more reserved, and could never be so entertaining, or outspoken, nor could she find a *bonmot* instantly, precisely, and without premeditation.

Alexa's marriage was solid, her husband a good and loving man. They shared everything: worries, joys, expenses, dreams, childrearing, common colds and housework. He did a great many things , which men of Katharina's generation considered women's work, and would not dream of touching while their wives had a blood pressure and pulse, never mind how low. Gary was the ideal husband and father. They probably had their marital squabbles like everyone else, but they resolved them on their own, and Alexa never complained.

Their daughters turned out amazingly well. True, Karen's brief, but stormy marriage shattered before they completed furnishing their house, and it was a painful shock to all of them. Deeply hurt, she moved back home, piled her share of the furniture into the basement of her parents, and licked her wounds in the old white–and–blue room of her younger years. But in the end, made of the same resilient material her mother and grandmother were made, she would rebound and give life another chance.

Laura, the younger daughter of Alexa, was breezing through her last year of undergraduate studies in biology and chemistry, after which she would start medical school in preparation for her life goal to do medical research.

But Katharina was somewhat unsure about her daughter. Alexa, although probably really tired, had no tragedies in her life, and no more troubles than the average workingwoman. She was just being funny, when she dashed off that note. Or was she?

While it was her daughter's personal style to cover up all her personal problems, Alexandra *did* carry a heavy load, even if she chose to show the world an upbeat, "nobody can get me down" face. Her job was unquestionably demanding with a great deal of responsibilities and many hours of work. The results of Gary's last medical checkup were not all that fabulous, and Dr. Ed warned her to take good care of her husband. She worried about Karen, and about everything else, even if she appeared to make light of every bad turn in her life. Close to fifty, the wear and tear of years started to show. She could still skillfully camouflage it, but the mother's eyes already detected the damage done by the years. Yes, she could be under a lot of stress and in need of help. Katharine missed the warning signs in Martin's health; she was not about to do that same mistake with Alexa.

She walked to the phone and called her daughter.

"Mom," Alexa exclaimed. "What happened? Did you break a leg, or did you have a coronary?"

"Why?"

"You usually don't call me at work."

"My question cannot wait. I want to know now what keeps you from spending some time on the beach, barefooted."

"Aha. It is not a coronary. It is Alzheimer. I was afraid of that all along. You already forgot that you have two granddaughters! One is nursing her shattered soul, and if I know Karen, her solution would be to enroll in graduate school to get over the hurt. The other is already bleeding us white with college expenses, and I cannot see an end of it. Also, I can't just hang a shield on my office door 'due to good weather gone fishing'. It is not in our budget right now to walk barefoot."

"Nonsense. You didn't take a vacation last year either. What is your exalted position worth if you cannot take what is due to even the lowliest member of your outfit? Darling, you don't live to work; you work to live. And remember, your father left you a bundle of money, which makes you independently wealthy. Go find an island for yourself. The money is there, waiting to be spent."

"I know, Mom. But I don't feel right about blowing it. It should really be yours."

"We have gone through this several times already. Apparently not I, but you are the one having some senior moments. Martin, and also your father, provided for me so well, that I probably can't spend a fraction of it before the almighty lid closes over my stiff form. I am more than 'comfortably situated', as polite people usually refer to the financial state of others. I don't need it; you do. Your father wanted it this way. I appreciated your humor in the last e-mail, but my sensitive, motherly ears picked up a note, and it sounds alarming to me."

"What did your motherly ears hear, pray, tell me!"

"I believe that you *really* are tired and that you *really* need to take it easy for a time, before one of the over-strained strings in your emotional or physical makeup snaps. Stress can do horrible things to a body. Think about it, will you? And if you don't want to take Gary's mother along, it is just as well. By the way, I know a place just right for the great escape."

"You are wonderful, and I am an idiot. I should never have sent that note to you. I should have known how you would react. With all your alarm systems clanging. You are a magnificent woman in every sense of the word, but a bit too intense, if you know what I mean to say ever so politely. There is also a less polite word for your condition, but I won't say it, because you raised me well. I really am OK, although I admit, at times I am quite exhausted, for no apparent reason."

"As I said before, you are overworked, and you are your own slave driver."

"And you are overreacting. I work a lot, but then everybody else is. So I am tired. Everybody is. I just feel the strain a bit more intensely than other women do. I suppose it is age, or the menopause, or something similar you doctors tell your patients when you can't come up with a decent diagnosis. I hoped the note would make you laugh, and as a bonus while writing it I released some of the strange tension I feel nowadays."

"This is what I am trying to tell you, dear; you are enduring a lot of responsibilities and tensions; this is not good for you."

"Life is quite strenuous, Mom."

"Tell me about it…"

"Mom, quit worrying. I am not under more stress than most working-women. I had no idea my note would disturb you this much. Had I known, I would have deleted it immediately, and then eaten three slices of chocolate cake to comfort me, instead of sending the garbage on to you. Forget it. I am OK."

"You already said that."

"Because it is true."

"'The lady doth protest too much, methinks'. Also, lately you started to lie about your age, but I happen to know the exact date, since I was present at your birth. Therefore, I know that you are far too old for me to tell you what to do. But for old time's sake promise to think about it. You need to rest to prevent illness. Promise that you will lighten the load in your life."

"I will. In my spare time."

"I love you."

"I suspected it all the time."

The sun was gone and suddenly the house felt chilly. Chilly and far too big and complex for a lonely woman. She wandered aimlessly through the richly furnished rooms into the kitchen, more out of habit than anything else. It was soon suppertime, but she lost her appetite nine months ago. The kitchen gleamed in the frigid splendor of a place not used for much any more. She loved to cook while Martin sat at the breakfast counter and talked to her. He knew how to amuse her. He poured the wine into tall glasses, and talked about his day, which seemed always more entertaining than the workday of other people. Or he would tell her about a wild plan, or talk to her about a new book.

They both loved to read; as a matter of fact they devoured books. Whenever a book appealed to both of them, which happened often enough, they bought it, although seldom read it again. Buying books was simply a fierce need to possess them. They absorbed the mood and the thoughts a book offered at the first reading, and were aware that their horizons expanded through it. But just as they never visited the same vacation spot a second time, because it would not be the same, and most likely not better, by the same logic they seldom returned to books once read. There were so many others, not yet discovered.

They were obsessive about their collection and never lent a book, not even to the dearest of friends. If somebody wanted to borrow one, Katharine promptly bought it as a gift for the person.

"My religion prohibits lending books. I don't share my husband, my toothbrush and my books with anyone," she declared with a smile, but everyone knew that she was dead serious on all three issues. Their library was a living testimonial to their taste; the shelves housed their preferences, and spoke of shared memories.

At times they bought a book on the strength of enthusiastic recommendation from others, or because it has stubbornly stayed on the best–seller list. Sometimes they were lucky and picked up a real gem this way, but mostly they realized that the successful book too often reflected the taste of the masses rather than their own.

"The world is bored out of its mind," Martin said at one time. The denigration of literature was one of the issues he could never let go without a comment. "For entertainment the masses crave excitement, brutality, and wish to vicariously indulge in crimes, which they are too timid to commit themselves. In addition they want to read about the kind of sex, which never was part of the human experience, let alone of their own. This is the reason why it is called fiction. There are plenty of talented authors, not geniuses to be sure but gifted enough, who are willing to serve the lucrative market. By using a reliable formula, they deliver quantities of trash, and the masses are happy. And so literature is sacrificed daily at the altar of the trivial and vulgar god of hard cash. No wonder most intelligent readers consistently turn to non–fiction."

"And of course this does not bother most people, except devoted eccentrics."

"Of course." But the books, which they considered inferior, were never placed on their shelves.

"Are we perhaps addicted?" she once asked in jest.

"Of course, we are. How else would you explain our dependence? I saw you once exhibit grave withdrawal symptoms when you were stuck without a book in a traffic jam."

"Of course, you exaggerate. Were you there in the car? If so, then how could I have been craving for a mere book? Do I ever have any distracting needs when I am with you?" She smiled at him with a devotion, which made them feel warm and close.

"Your logic is frightening. I can see why men are afraid of smart women. Your kind can blow away our carefully built superiority, and do it with amazing speed and efficiency."

Yes, they loved books, and while she was not particularly keen to do housework, she always dusted the hundreds of volumes in their library with a sense of gentle, almost sensual delight.

Katharina, standing in the unused kitchen, remembered Alexa's wish of not having to cook when she did not feel like it, and sighed. Gladly would she cook for the gourmet that he was, but hunger was a thing of the past. They lost their appetites at the same time: he, because of his illness; she, because of the worry about him. Nevertheless, it was expected of her to continue living, and nourishment was necessary to stay alive. She settled for more tea and toast.

The evening would be long and empty, and it had to be filled with something before sleep would bring welcome release. She would read. That always offered temporary escape. She stepped into the cozy library, but instead of choosing a book, sat down at the small desk placed by the window. Her diary was there, open, but for long weeks she made no new entries.

Just after Martin's death she wrote furiously and mostly incoherently, to get over an overpowering sense of guilt. She blamed herself for not noticing earlier how ill he was, for not insisting more aggressively that he visit a doctor right away. Precious time was wasted. What sort of a physician was she when she could not detect the alarming signs in her own husband? He refused to accept what he must have known at some level, and she was far too eager to believe his lighthearted explanations. When he finally sought help, it was too late.

Even worse memories haunted her. During those harrowing months while he was dying, there were times when she too reached the end of her rope. Once she was driving home after doing some errands, and the reality of his condition hit her with such brutal force that she started to cry in the car, and ended up screaming, "It cannot be. I can't take it, I can't. I can't." After she lost her voice because of the senseless screaming, and there were no more tears left, she knew that she behaved ridiculously.

She moaned like a sick child for several miles before totally exhausted she reached her home.

After this outburst, when she visited him in the evening at the hospital, she was her own self again. But he no longer was the Martin she knew and loved. He was cranky, complaining, irritable and found fault with everything. It was a grotesque division of labor. He had the pain and the certitude that it is all over; she had the anxiety, the stress, the fear for him, the exhaustion and the enormous emotional burden of having to face an altered life. He suffered physically, and the reality of his body filled his every agonizing moment; her terror was not dulled by physical pain and discomfort. It hit her square and neat.

She hoped that her occasional unhappy and destructive thoughts did not show, because she was ashamed of her unkind and selfish feelings, regretted the silent arguments with him, and praised the grace of the Creator for not letting the secret thoughts and unworthy emotions of man be printed out for everybody to see. The human soul can sink into frightful abysses, which would shock all decent people, who are far too ready to assure the world that they never have ugly thoughts at all. Katharina did. She regretted them, never really indulged in them for long, but at times her own impatience and bitterness did surface, because it had to. It was painful when it happened, and almost unbearable in retrospect. She used to pray alternately for a miracle for him and angelic patience for herself.

She opened the diary randomly and read with deep astonishment what she wrote on a lonely night.

"*Today Martin is not doing well. Neither physically nor emotionally. I try to understand his pain, and to imagine how I would face the verdict he has to face. Probably with far less courage than he does. But the truth is that he is making me not only sad, but angry too, and I feel guilty about it. My occasional negative thoughts make me into a bad person, even though I was trained to know that such emotions can and do surface in the caregiver.*

He is so ill; we both know this. I try to give him everything he needs at this time; yet, he seems so very dissatisfied, critical and aggressive about my ministrations. But I too am under a great deal of pressure. True, my troubles are minimal in comparison to his, but still, I am hurting, and am in desperate need of a good word, a smile, anything to show that he understands. Does he not know that I too am grieving and will be grieving for a long time to come? He has no priority over the pain; this tragedy touches us both.

His impatience, his total absorption with himself and with all the physical symptom he has, makes me want to scream. I want to shake him to become again the man he used to be, and want the assurance that we will soon continue to live as before. I am angry that this had to happen to us. It is not his fault, but I blame everything and everybody, God and Martin included.

I don't completely sink into this destructive mind–set, but I cannot deny that I have those ugly thoughts. Mea culpa, mea maxima culpa. If I do have to face this horror, why couldn't God at least make me to be like Florence Nightingale? Martin tells his doctors too little, and to me too much. I cannot help him, and I wonder if he realizes how much I love him and how this is hurting and burdening me. Is it self–pity? Am I sorry for myself, for poor Katharina, who will never be again with the man she loves so very much? Are the tears for him or for me? I think for both of us. Fate did a really cruel thing to us.

He wants to come home, which I understand. I would want the same thing in similar circumstances. But it is not possible for me to give him the 24–hour sophisticated care he is receiving at the hospital. It would be irresponsible to move him home and certainly his doctors, with the exception of Ed, would advise against it. But he blames me for denying his wish, and there was almost a hint of hatred in him when I again told him to be a bit patient and understanding. He lashed out at me and defined patience. He was right and I cried all the way home.

And I don't know what to do. How does it feel to be a prisoner in a hospital room, exposed, poked, suctioned, pricked and hurt in all the ways a well equipped torture chamber offers? How would I feel if I had to spend my last days among clicking machines, gurgling life supports, tubes down my throat, in my veins while I fight awful spasms of nausea and the even worse attacks of pain, of fear, and of loneliness? I too would want to leave it all, and come home to the place I love and to the one, who gives me security and warmth. And in that case, he would bring me home. He would not let me suffer alone, and would carry me home even if a thousand dragons stood in his way. Why can't I do the same for him? No wonder he will die hating me.

I had a strange dream the other night. More and more I do believe that somehow dreams run parallel to life, but they appear in a distorted way, so that we only rarely understand them. Dreams are not foretelling the future – they reflect the present. If we pay attention to our daily life, we can fully understand our dreams. Or in reverse: our dreams mirror our innermost feelings and unresolved conflicts.

I dreamt that I was at the bank of a river. I heard some alarming noises from behind and as I turned I saw a horde of enemy soldiers rush toward me. Their closed, dark faces were void of passion; I could only see cruelty and determination. These were barely human beings, and I could not expect mercy from them. I knew suddenly that I was in terrible danger. These soldiers were about to rape me, and then kill me after. There was no way for me to escape, and I was totally paralyzed with fear. As I looked up I saw Martin in the distance. He lifted a gun – and shot me. Not the soldiers, but me. There were too many of them and they had the power and every advantage, and nothing and nobody could stop them from doing this awful violence to me. Martin seemed to understand that he could not chase away the masses, so he did the only merciful thing he could do to save me: he killed me. I died in my sleep and was happy.

I woke up then, infinitely grateful and full of love, because I knew this man would never let any sort of harm, or unspeakable horror come to me, even if he would have to kill me to avert the terror. I would always be totally safe with him.

But upon awakening the thin fabric of dream is predictably torn, and I no longer knew which was the woof, and which the warp. And then, as rationality returned, I realized that the enemy soldiers weren't what I first thought them to be: they were not even humans, but they were the cancer cells, our mutual and deadly enemies. According to the perverted, confused pattern of the resting mind, which during sleep temporarily divorces itself from rationality, I was made to believe that the enemy was about to attack me; however, in the sober morning I realized the mistake of reversal: they were not at all interested in me, only in him. But unlike him, I am no hero. I hesitate and waver, and do not have the courage to save him from the thing he fears. But he! He would always have the courage to raise his rifle.

His courage and the magnitude of his love, both very real and not just in dream pictures, are the gifts which will keep me going long after he is gone.

Meanwhile I am facing his pleading, his needs, all contradicting my beliefs and the things common sense dictates to me. I am a doctor and do not know how to handle a gun. I swore to save lives, not to destroy them. But he cannot accept that.

How am I to know what is best for him?

In a reverse situation, just like in my dream, he would know. He always knows what to do. He never doubts, when real issues have to be decided."

She sighed and was grateful that the negative and destructive thoughts screaming at her from the pages only surfaced once in a while, and that instead of speaking them out loud, she confined them to the patient pages of the diary. At the same time she wondered how those caregivers coped, who had not months, but years of this to bear, like Ed Collins.

In the end, against the better judgment of his doctors and against her own common sense, her heart won the battle, and she did bring him home from the hospital. He was happy, but she felt woefully inadequate. It did not help that she used to be a practicing pediatrician, hence had extensive medical training. Even the generous help of the hospice team and the daily presence of their closest friend, Dr. Ed Collins, did not ease her insecurity. She was doctor enough to blindly place her trust in whirring, clicking, sophisticated life supports, and never lost the conviction that it is the holy duty of doctors to keep a patient alive at all costs, and as long as possible.

Martin was of a different opinion. He wanted peace, tranquility and dignity, refused all invasive and painful interventions and only asked for painkillers and to be left alone.

"Why insult the body with every imaginable torture and discomfort just for the sake of adding a few days or hours? Why make the end of our life intolerably painful and lonely? I had a good, rewarding life, and I want to let it go with peace and gratitude, in dignity and close to the one I love. You doctors believe you can fool Nature and foil God's intent. How wrong you are! In the end, despite all your devilish efforts, death will come as usual, although it will indeed be a bit delayed. You might think your intervention is noble, but I for one would not thank you for it."

After she brought him home, he never once complained, and never regretted his decision. Although weak and easily fatigued, he was almost his old self. It was almost unbelievable, but at times he felt good and strong, free of pain.

"I thank you," he said simply after she helped him into the recliner in the winter garden where he could enjoy the solar heat and the lush plants. "I won't be here to help you when your time comes, but I hope that you too will find an unusual person, who has the grace to do what you are doing for me now."

She held his thin, cold and wasted hand in hers, and did not know whether she should be grateful for his calm acceptance, or should break down sobbing, because obviously, he has given up the fight for his life. In the end she did neither.

"I keep having such interesting and intensive dreams," he told her after she cleared away his lunch, which he barely touched. "There were a few people in my life whom I did not really like, and there were others, especially while I practiced law, who actively disliked me, and did me much harm. Like that skunk, Bill Jones.

"I dream of them now, and they all appear extremely beautiful, elegant and happy in my dreams. Why is that so? Are they no longer angry with me – or are they happy that I am exiting? Or did I already cease to exist for them, and so they can shed their ugly hatred; therefore, they appear beautiful and good again? Do some of us have to die so that others can get rid of their destructive hatreds? I am not sure that it makes sense."

She listened silently, holding his hand. He was trying to get used to the idea of death, and while her wish was to make him happy during the last stretch of his life, she no longer felt that false hopes are coins with which tranquility could be purchased.

He often had frightening dreams of missing a train, a plane or an appointment. This was strange, because they both were always and everywhere on time; they never missed appointments, and were never late for even insignificant occasions. He told her once that being punctual is the politeness practiced by royalty and this became his personal creed. As in everything else, she adapted herself to his ideal. Friends often teased them that watches and clocks could be set by their arrivals,—they were that punctual in their appearances. Yet in his dreams he was continually trying to be on time while he was lost in endless byways and complications, and was late, left behind and was frustrated.

At other times he was dreaming of food, delicious food, wonderful fruits and a rich selection of breads.

"Why would I dream of festive dinner tables and rich food when I can barely keep down a piece of toast? What is the meaning of all this food in my dreams? Happiness of past times haunting me at a most inappropriate time? Am I recalling the pleasure when we had friends for dinner? Or am I simply acting out something in my dream, which I no longer can do in life?"

And once again she sat silently at his bedside and tried not to think of the barely touched lunch. The rich tables of the past were no more than memories. She was grateful whenever he managed a scant half cup of bouillon.

The time came, when he was too weak to receive visitors and could not even take calls. Their friends were concerned, loving, but he no longer had the strength to listen to their false encouragements, or tearful farewells. She stopped picking up the phone –the answering machine stored the messages and it was easier this way. If she talked to the well–meaning friends they were full of advice, ideas and empty words. She appreciated the intent, but decided that life is easier without it. She was weary of everybody telling her what to do and how to feel. Only Alexa, with her incredible sensitivity and common sense was able to give the support and warmth she needed.

He died in her arms on a dismal late March evening.

Katharina closed the diary, chose a book and then turning off the lights as she went through her ornate home retired for another night of troubled sleep.

TWO

As a chilly autumn wind swept through the city, Katharina stepped into Miss Emily's Tea Room, where she was to meet her three good friends for lunch.

They have known each other for a long time, their husbands were good friends, and they spent many happy hours together. After they were left alone their widowhood, common sorrows, and shared problems brought them even closer. Like birds in a heavy storm, they held together.

Susan was the first to lose her husband; he died in a car crash. In the following years three of the remaining husbands were victims of cancer or clogged arteries. The women left behind coped as best they could. They involved themselves in activities, which they hoped were of some small benefit to mankind, and which also helped to fill the void. And of course, they relied on each other for comfort. They were good looking, but no longer glamorous, with the exception of Susan; were untitled, except for Katharina's MD., and never made the society pages. They were also brave, honest women in semi–sensible shoes, clad in suits with quiet accessories, and suffering silently from thinning bones, and from the uninvited hooligan, arthritis. Passing them on the street they would probably not be noticed, because age, annoying to society, was stamped on their faces. Fate has forgotten to give them the compensation of a luminous aura to show their inner gentleness and goodness, and their heroic struggle to accept the truncated emotional life left to them.

Their friendship was precious and comforting, and they supported each other during personal ordeals. Even during the worst of times a shared lunch, or a quick visit was a benediction on their otherwise difficult life. After a personal tragedy hit one of them, they would shy away from public places, and preferred each other's homes for their visits, but as the wounds slowly healed they again ventured out into the world. Give or take a few years, they were close to the seventh decade. Although all four were exceptionally healthy and active, the remaining energies had to be frugally used; therefore, they preferred to meet in restaurants, and let the professionals do the cooking and the cleaning up.

At the beginning the luncheons were organized to celebrate a birthday or other special event, such as Sarah's first bifocals, or Lettie's decision to enroll in an art class. Eventually the luncheon meetings became regular events.

From all the places they loved the Tea Room best. It had a genteel, purposefully old–world atmosphere. The furniture was antique and expensively shabby; embroidered, or quilted pillows on easy chairs next to robust houseplants, an abundance of fruits in pewter bowls, old dolls in wicker carriages, a basket with yarn and knitting needles lent it a homey look, and lace curtains, tied back with silk rosebuds completed the illusion. It was more like the country home of an aged aunt, who did not have the heart to throw away anything, than an exclusive eatery in a metropolitan area. Above and beyond the old–fashioned décor it also offered light and delicious food. As soon as Katharina entered, she spotted Sarah and Lettie at their favorite table next to the fireplace.

"Hello to both of you," she greeted them. "It is good to see you healthy and smiling. And this fire feels like a therapeutic blessing on my aching bones. The miserable, wet weather lets all the demons loose in my joints and bones."

"You are not alone, and hello to you too. Susan is late, as is her irritating habit. We ordered a pot of tea to keep us pacified while we wait for her. Hopefully she'll make it before the place closes." Sarah, as usually, spoke for both of them. "The cream of broccoli soup was highly recommended by the waitress, but we won't order, unless Susan is more than twenty minutes late."

"She isn't late, Sarah; we are all early."

"That's beside the point."

"The broccoli soup sounds tempting." Katharina was trying to change the subject and soothe Sarah.

"It is creamy and has grated Parmesan cheese added to it," Lettie, catching her friend's intent, informed.

"And all of it will eventually be added to my expanding waistline."

Dieting, like the weather, is always a good starter for conversation among women in general, but since Sarah was fighting a losing battle with her weight, the topic was never ignored.

"Diets drive me insane," she now complained. "I'm a vegetarian and because I do not eat any meat, people think that I should not have a problem with my weight. But if I take the formula of a basic one hundred pounds for five feet of height, and add five pounds for every inch above it, then I'm almost fifty pounds overweight."

"Sarah, you don't look overweight," Lettie argued.

"You are very kind, but this does not change a thing. I am fat. On my last medical checkup I glanced into the papers, and it said, 'sixty–eight year old obese woman…' Pow! I reeled and was deeply insulted. To call me obese! It has such a terribly mortifying sound to it."

"Some people just simply gain weight, when they get older. We move less, and when we do, we do it slower than once upon a time. Our metabolism works differently, not to speak of the muscles and hormones."

"You said it. This is all so true, but does not console me. Since the age of twenty–five I gained steadily a few pounds a year, but somehow didn't notice it until recently. I habitually look at other fat women and think rather smugly, 'Not me! Heavens, not me, and shame on them.' My body image lagged about twenty years and fifty pounds behind reality. Now here I am, succumbing to a wretched state of depression. I'm fat, gloomy, unpleasant and frustrated, because I am hungry most of the time, and am also fully aware that I'll never be able to lose fifty pounds and keep it off."

"Would you really like to be thin? Are you convinced that my bones are more attractive than your fat?" asked Lettie.

"Definitely. However, I don't crave the emaciated look, but would just like to avoid the stuffed sack shape. And if possible, I would like to see my toes once in a while."

"You exaggerate, of course, but on the other hand, you know what they say. Cut out fats, sweets, carbs, alcohol, and exercise more. Ask Katharina. Doctors know best."

"I know those answers and hate them all. You don't have to spell them out. I want to live well and be slim without any effort and pain on my part."

"Can't be done, unless you inherited fantastic genes."

"I know that. I am also not motivated enough to lose weight, mostly because the goal seems overwhelming. Perhaps my taste buds are unhappy and cry out in anguish, when they are made to face another dish of low fat cottage cheese, or another bowl of salad *nada*. 'No salad without dressing' is my revised Bostonian battle cry. Carrot sticks without a nice creamy, dippy sauce are enough to drive me off the diet and make me commit suicide in a bowl of creamed broccoli soup. And then I think, what for, and the hell with it. Cheesecake is what soothes the aching soul. And if possible, serve with it a nice cup of strong hot coffee with sweetened, cold whipping cream on top. That is what real sensual pleasures are made of, at least at my age."

"Which age? You are at this moment not acting your own," Katharina said, but softened her remark with a smile.

"But I am. I really am. I am at the age of relentless compromises, and I act accordingly. Consider how the horizons of sexuality, hope for attractiveness, for fun and games have shrunk during the last decades! To compensate I get what I can, and where I can get it. Cheesecake is about all that is left. It will have to do. And than consider this: after fifty you have to make a decision about which you'll favor more: your derrière or your face. You can't serve both. Lose fifty pounds at our age and you'll again fit into a size twelve pair of pants, but your face could be easily mistaken for a shriveled prune. Toss a coin and see. And don't distract me from my comfortable and rightful misery."

"Sarah, you sound like virtue gone to seed."

"Hogwash, my precious. I sound like virtue facing reality."

"Have it your way, but don't fret too much. You are OK."

After the diets, the weather, the other trivia was discussed, and then Lettie turned to Katharina, the most recent widow.

"I am not trying to pry…"

"I know Lettie. Thanks for asking. I am fine."

"A graceful inquiry and a graceful answer," mumbled Sarah. "This exchange is so gracious that it totally lacks meaning. This brings to mind a nice pile of buffalo shit, also known—at least by the polite segment of our society—as television programming, You must know that due to a fatal weakness in my character, I thoroughly enjoy watching disaster movies on the TV…"

"Are we still discussing Katharina?" Lettie asked. Sarah had a way of getting off the subject and never returning to it again.

"We are, just have a little patience. Anyhow, as I was saying, for some reason it comforts me to see such condensed forms of disaster. My own troubles appear minimal in comparison. I rather like to see the world in flames. However the story always gets to a point of unpardonable idiocy just after the world has partially crashed. I get so vexed that I would like to hit the TV with the first convenient vase. Picture this: New York is undergoing the greatest natural catastrophe moviemakers are capable of inventing. Violent series of earthquakes shake the city, volcanoes erupt – in downtown New York no less – buildings collapse and those that are still standing are burning with vengeance, but very picturesquely. The heroine, with hair and makeup intact except for a few rather cute smudges, is stuck in the metro, which has been partially flattened by falling debris. Or flooded. Or enveloped in smoke – take your pick. There are corpses left and right, the wall of fire, or water, is moving closer, her broken leg is wedged under the twisted remains of a seat; she is choking from smoke, is parched from heat, or whatever the plot demands; the boulders above her are shifting menacingly, ready to crash every second; she does not know where her two school age children are at the moment; her home has been demolished beyond recognition. At this catastrophic moment the hero, most likely through divine interference and by using his uncanny skills and stamina, reaches the mangled car underground. Ignoring the carnage around them, or her painfully wedged leg, with trembling hands smoothes the locks from her anguished face and asks in a tone of true love, 'Are you all right?' The idiot! A more dim–witted question could not be formulated by an entire committee of imbeciles, yet in every disaster movie somebody asks this at least once in a similar situation, and of course, she always answers that she is all right. The world is about to go under, but thank you, she is just fine."

"And the moral of the story?" inquired Lettie with a hint of impatience.

"No moral to it. It is just so unreal to ask someone how she is, and expect her to answer, 'Just fine, thank you,' at the time when her world just shattered."

"I meant no harm," Lettie said, obviously hurt.

"We know that, Lettie. But I am getting on, really I am," said Katharina defending her friend from the sharp tongue of Sarah. "Perhaps I would be worse off if I did not have Alexandra, but she keeps my head above water. And of course, without your friendship, the world would be very bleak indeed." Yes, there was pain, and lots of it, but no longer any terror. Terror raged during all those weeks and days before it actually happened. When she asked herself every morning, would this be his last day? Is this our last Sunday together?

They fell silent for a moment, and then Lettie spoke again. "We all deal so differently with what life was pleased to hand us." Indeed, they were.

Lettie was a gifted artist, and she painted relentlessly as if she wanted to catch up with all what she missed while being a perfect wife, and never had the time to live for herself. Susan was the model grandmother: a caring, always ready babysitter, creative entertainer of children, fairy godmother, Santa Claus, Tooth Fairy and lovely provider of perfect holiday dinners, all rolled in one. No wonder her family adored her.

Sarah was outspoken with a cynical edge to her views, while she was aggressively filling her days with activities. A top manager in a multibillion dollar outfit could not be busier than she was. She was indiscriminate in what she did. Some of her activities were truly good works; at other times she was merely a busybody for some bagatelle cause. The goal was to be always on the go. The high energy she expended blocked out what hurt her most.

Katharina was still in limbo.

Out of consideration for each other the topics they discussed usually did not touch their personal losses, but the question of how to arrange the future, what to do, how to fill the long days from breakfast to bedtime was an often repeated topic.

"I refuse to become a basket case any time soon," Sarah said. "The secret is to keep busy. Are you still painting up a storm, Lettie?"

"In every spare moment; of which I have lots. It is a wonderful tranquilizer." They knew that Katharina was still drifting in an unsettled way and did not yet have a focused goal in her life. Because they were always discreet and mindful of easily bruised emotions, they quickly changed the subject.

"You are lucky with Alexa," Sarah said now. "My Marisa is a different sort altogether. I can't say she neglects me. She is not that crude. She'd call, or breeze in unannounced for the shortest visit ever recorded in history. She chats and her smile is brilliant as she repeats her mantra of how well I look and how wonderful it is that I am so active and outgoing. Then she reminds me that in case I should start slowing down, I ought to consider moving into a home. She plays the ostrich and prefers not to see what she does not want to see. I am supposed to stay strong and independent for her sake. She likes her comfortable life and the fascination she gets from regularly changing her husbands. She does not want my eventual senility and fragility to disturb her smooth sailing. The recurrent theme of her song is that if I slow down I'll be sent to my room, in translation: to a home for the aged. Not that I would ever want her help, but it is so terribly superfluous to keep reminding me to count her out when the chips will be down. You are indeed lucky with Alexandra."

Katharina was instantly vexed, because she hated when people thought it was through luck that Alexandra turned out to be such a wonderful daughter. It was not luck. It took a lot of work, understanding, guidance, sacrifices, and a warm, loving home to make her into what she was. However, her vexation quickly evaporated. Sarah was hurting. She was perhaps the most lonely among the four of them. Susan's children and grandchildren offered warmth and a degree of security to her. They were always around, caring, loving; their generosity was touching. Lettie had her art. Sarah only had the selfish coldness of Marisa. Katharina riveted her attention on her tea and did not comment.

"I guess children want to live their own life. So did we, when it was our turn," Lettie remarked. She was quiet by nature, and after she lost her husband, she lived for her art only. It consoled her and filled her days. She did not have any children and for a while after his death she was completely withdrawn. Their marriage was good, but she lived for and through her husband with a dependence that was pathological, according to Sarah. No wonder she was lost without him. Yet, in the end she pulled herself together, although the path she chose was lonely. Other then the lunches with her three friends, she did not seem to keep in touch with anyone else. Katharina often wondered how she managed to sell her paintings. Perhaps she had some sort of a business manager, who did the transactions. She never spoke of these things. After her husband's death she sold the big elegant Mediterranean condo in the center of the city, and moved to the outskirt into a tiny century–old home. It had a picket fence and a garden, comfortable furniture, a lovely view of the hills, and there was a small lake on the property. She converted the workshop attached to the back of the house into a studio, packed away her designer clothes, chose comfortable slacks and shirts and at complete peace with the world painted her landscapes and variations of fruits and flowers.

"Of course we were all rearing to be independent," remarked Sarah morosely. "I for one could barely wait to leave the nest. However, it never occurred to me to turn back from the door and kick my parents in the teeth as a tender farewell. Nowadays this seems quite a fashionable way to leave the parental house."

"Sarah, don't be so gloomy. This is not the common way." As always, Lettie was ready with a band–aid to cover up the hurt. There was a short, awkward pause and finally Katharina broke it with an answer to Lettie's question in the hope of steering the conversation away from the gloomy topic.

"I know that soon I should make some decisions about the life I'll live from now on. I guess that was the reason for Lettie's question. I can't continue pretending that everything will go on as it did before. Some changes are inevitable. I have to find a closure and a new content for my life. Susan has her family, Sarah her good works, Lettie her painting and contemplative life – but Katharina is still scratching pointlessly in the same place, like the needle of an old phonograph, which reached the end of the song," she said, and was quiet for a moment, then added ruefully, "I could not even sort out Martin's closets yet. Everything is as it was."

"Don't rush a thing, Kathy," Sarah said with unusual softness in her voice. "You are not yet in control and if you make an irrevocable decision now, soon enough there will be the devil at your door to collect payments."

"Your house is so very large for just one person," remarked Lettie. "You have no idea how wonderful it is to clean a small place like mine, in an hour with time to spare. My place is a cozy one–person house, but who needs more? I have come to the conclusion that hanging on to the past is unhealthy. I can't turn back the clock, nor make events unhappen, so I trudge along as best as I can."

For a moment it seemed that conversation, because it wandered into tricky territory, was stuck. Katharina's house was large to be sure, and packed with treasured items collected through the years. Every piece, just like their books, carried a memory, and she knew she could never part with any of it. It was also a nightmare to clean. Her recurring fear was that one day Rosie, her household help, would leave her, and she would be stuck with far too many rooms to clean, far too many art objects and books to dust, and endless stretches of oak floors to polish, oriental rugs to vacuum, draperies to clean. Lettie had a valid point, but a point not acceptable to Katharina.

"I know what you mean. Both of you. There are moments I want to close my home and flee from it, but almost at the same moment I know I couldn't do it. Not yet. Or perhaps never," she admitted with a sigh.

"Where would you go?"

"If I had all the money in the world?"

"Let us assume."

"To a place totally different from the place where I lived with Martin. So different in fact, that I would not just acquire a new home, but start a new life as well."

"A profitable beginning, but cut the philosophy and name a concrete place," Sarah had no patience with trimmings. She wanted the bare facts, the faster the better.

"Lord Rothschield's and Lady Serena's place at Corfu," Katharina said after she thought about it for a moment.

"Lord knows, you are not humble. As a matter of fact your wish borders on megalomania," Sarah mumbled, but could not derail Katharina.

"The space, the colors, the vistas, the magnificent simplicity of it speak to me," she said. "And I love water. The bigger and the bluer it is, so much the better. That place has it all. It must be the closest approximation to heaven."

"I suppose you have been invited to stay there at times," teased Sarah.

"Of course. Every other weekend."

"I didn't mean quite that much money, my dear. Could you come down many notches on the income level until you reach the amount mortals make? What would you choose then?" Lettie asked.

"You said money was not a problem. But have it your way; I'll choose another one," she answered after just the briefest hesitation. "I once saw photos of a house John Lautner designed somewhere around Los Angeles. It must have been terribly expensive, but certainly not as much as what Lord Jacob paid for his dramatic hideaway with his outsized swimming pool carved right into a marble quarry. Am I allowed to choose that?"

Lettie magnanimously agreed.

"The house appealed to me more than any other house I ever saw, except that of Lord Rothschield. Lautner worked with huge, open spaces, soaring walls, angled roofs, lots of glass, concrete–aggregate materials, no right angles anywhere, whimsical spatial solutions, water around the structure reflecting the light, and oddly spaced apertures in the waffled ceiling admitting light in whimsical patterns. Everything very simple, uncluttered, and dramatic. Lovely earth tones, and not a single object to detract from the magnificence of the architecture. A house to die for. And just like the Corfu place, this too was built in and around Nature, without any distractions. I kept the magazine for years. It was a treat just to look at the photos."

"You could commission an architect to build something like it for you."

"Yes, I could. But would I want to?" Katharina answered. "Sometimes I really think that I'd want something like it, and can even imagine myself in those graceful spaces. I can almost see the uncomplicated, almost ascetic life in these big, simplified areas, surrounded by light, shapes, Nature, pure elegance and little else. No paintings, no art objects, no cozy corners, no secluded private nooks, no memories, because uncluttered simplicity is the very point of that house. I know that. So I would have to leave behind all what we collected, all the objects rich with memories. Perhaps I could do it. Perhaps. But then there are the books."

"Yes, the books would pose a problem," agreed Lettie.

"Naturally, I could not part with those. I would need a study or library somewhere in the big house, closed off from the rest of the areas to house them. However the concept of continuous open spaces would be instantly violated with my uninspired botchwork. Can you see that? On the other hand, I could hang some of our most favorite paintings in this library–study…and a few of the art objects could be placed on the shelves…some Persian rugs with their vibrant colors… And before I know, I am cluttering up this architectural wonder the same as my present home is cluttered with the things I love. I actually pitched the magazine then, because I finally realized that it is not for me."

"As I so wisely said a minute ago: take it easy, give yourself time to see what you want. And then decide to do nothing." said Sarah.

The waitress was discreetly circling their table waiting for the orders, just when Susan finally swept in. She looked radiant and glamorous in a fawn colored suede ensemble and high–heeled boots; energy and happiness charged the air around her.

"What happened to you, Sweetie? Did you take a double dose of Geritol?" inquired Sarah. "You haven't looked this good since Eisenhower's presidency."

"I don't need Geritol just now," she bubbled. "Would you like to hear my news now, or after lunch?'

"I suggest a compromise. Let's save the last three nerves of our waitress and order first, then you tell us."

After carefully studying the menu, they chose what they always ended up having: soup, a salad, cheesecake for Sarah, and more tea. Sarah, although a vegetarian, never tried to convert anyone to her way of thinking, but the friends knew that the sight of meat offended her. Anyhow, they reached the age of diminishing appetite; soup and salad sounded good enough even when Sarah was not present.

"Are you ready for my news?" Susan asked. "I cannot really keep it any longer! Listen ladies, I'm getting married!"

Had she announced that the earth is flat, or that she inherited a million, or that she met an alien, she could not have shocked her three friends more.

"I suppose we heard it right," spoke Sarah. "There is not a chance of misunderstanding, is there?"

"Don't tell me you too are judging me insane!"

"Who gave you this shattering diagnosis?" asked Katharina, although she had a fairly good idea.

"My loving family. Every devoted member of it. They are up in arms and are of the opinion that I should be examined, locked up, or at least put under guardianship." Susan smiled a brittle smile, then continued. "They think it is indecent, and reiterate in so many words that my sacred duty is to remain the tragic widow and dignified matriarch for the rest of my life. Covertly they probably object to an aging parent, but overtly they declare war when said parent does not wish to be embalmed before clinical death sets in. My son said, 'how could you do this to us,' and my daughter said 'we won't have it'. Can you fathom this? Now please, don't you too look at me as if I lost my marbles."

Lettie was the first to gather her wits, and wished Susan the best, even before she asked for details, then the others followed, but the announcement left a painful hollowness in all three of them. After this marriage Susan would no longer fit into the established circle of widows. Her world has changed. She found a partner and would have no need for the support they gave to each other up to now. For better or for worse, she sailed into a safe harbor, while the rest of them, nursing one more loss, would be left out at sea. The good wishes were sincere, but the prospect of losing a member of their tight little group was cheerless. Sarah, in her rough manner expressed the sentiment, which they all felt, but hesitated to say, "Selfish bitches that we are, our first thoughts are about losing you. The good wishes come after that. We'll miss you terribly."

"But I'm not leaving you," Susan protested.

"But you are, old girl. You are," Sarah said. She appeared a shade gloomier than before.

The bowls of soup arrived, and as they shook out their napkins a welcome pause set in.

"My marriage with Julius was great, you know that," Susan said after they finished the meal, and the waitress filled the teacups again. "Perhaps I am wrong, but I believe that if your life has been miserable with a man, you would definitely avoid a new tie. Few of us are foolish enough to enter into a new affair, when the old one gave nothing but grief. "

"I buy that," Sarah interrupted.

"But when it was a good one, you will always miss the warmth, the companionship, the sharing. I did," Susan continued. "Up to now I could not find the mate I was looking for. In George I found him. By the way he is younger than I am. Not by much; he is as old as Julius was when he died."

"And you are happy?" Lettie said. It was not so much a question as a statement.

"Yes, very much so. Completely and peacefully, because of him. Unhappy and torn, because of the reaction of my children and grandchildren. They never said it out loud, but now it is obvious how they view people my age. In their eyes we have turned sexless, useless, powerless and marginally senile. When we express wishes, which are in opposition to what society expects from us, we are instantly viewed as disgusting, undignified, crazy, and somehow dirty. I always suspected that society is but a fossilized beast, but I was not prepared to hear the same scandalized outcry from my own family, who supposedly loved me so much."

"Fates have seen fit to punish us in choice ways, but the plague of society's tyranny, not to speak of the equal tyranny of our dearly beloved, is the most irritating and restricting of all the damned punitive measures," Sarah agreed.

"All this time I thought that my family was loving and understanding. And now they come up with arguments they dredged up from the Dark Ages. It baffles and hurts me."

"Yes, I understand," said Sarah. "The little buggers can be so self–centered that if egoism would be painful, they would scream to high heaven day and night. Don't do anything, which upsets their equilibrium, or their preconceived and provincial ideas about your role in life. Don't do anything to scandalize their no–brain friends. No matter how liberal they are in their own affairs, they are absolute fanatics about *your* morals and *your* desires. You step out of line and declare any sort of independence, and they get moral contractions."

Katharina was suddenly tired and wanted to be home, safely surrounded by the things, which still bound her to Martin. Her friends were obviously unhappy and she could not ease their pain. She could not even ease her own.

Lettie, in her new independence was lately more practical than the others, and she was the one to ask the final question.

"And when will this happen?"

"At our age, we can't afford to wait. Long engagements are for the young, or for those who are unsure."

"We know all that bunk," interrupted Sarah rather impatiently. "Tell us when."

"In three weeks."

There was silence. After the first announcement they knew that it would be happening, but not so soon. Some events, such as death, are unavoidable, but as long as these are somewhere in the nebulous future, a very long way off, their existence is not so disturbing.

"Very wise, considering that you are at the Medicare Plus One stage," agreed Sarah. "Have you discussed who is going to push whom in the wheelchair in the near future? Or are they now making them for two, like buggies for twins, or like tandem bicycles?"

"Age has nothing to do with this," Susan said defensively.

"Of course not. And we know that we are still young, even if the world does not seem to agree with us. Many women marry past the first bloom.

George Eliot for one. She was sixty–one," Katharina put in, then immediately wished to bite off her tongue. There were a lot of other women,
who could have been lined up as an example, but Eliot was a badly chosen,
sinister example, as she died barely seven months later in the same year she
married. Fortunately nobody caught the *faux pas*, and Katharina continued
in a light, teasing tone, "Years mean nothing. I can't swear to its accuracy,
but I think Homer wrote somewhere that women in Greece started to
count their age not from birth, but from the day they married."

"Oh yeah. And I also heard it say that time spent in combat counts
double. And isn't marriage a generalized combat? That would make Susan,
let's see, well over one hundred years old…"

"Shut up, Sarah," Lettie said with brief simplicity, and nodded to Susan
to continue.

"Because of our age, and because of the united resistance of my children,
we decided to go about it quietly, without fanfare. I would have liked to
share my joy with those I love, but the stars are in a very unfavorable
constellation." Susan was fighting those unwelcome tears, but then defiantly
turned from her pain and added,"We have never been to Hawaii, and it
seems to us the ideal place to start our new life together. We booked on
a ship on which we'll be married. We figure that people going on a great
vacation are relaxed and accepting, and they won't be scandalized, like my
children are. We'll stay in Hawaii a few weeks."

"Sounds delicious."

"It isn't what I really wanted, but it will have to do," Susan shrugged.
"Of course, I did not plan on the virginal white lace gown and veil, nor
bridesmaids, nor Lohengrin, but I would have loved my family and friends,
cases of Pommery, good food, and a good time shared. But, as it often
happens, we are forced to take plan B, and are sailing to Hawaii."

"Doesn't sound like a real punishment, but of course, you'll leave us out
of an event for which we might envy you to the point of intensive hatred,
while you engage in some delicious rumpy–humpy under the palm trees,"
said Sarah.

"You won't hate me. You are far too sophisticated for that. And our
friendship goes deeper than that." She elegantly ignored the remark about
the rumpy–humpy.

All the luncheon guests left already, and the waitress was hovering,
discreetly putting the place in order.

"Girls, methinks we better leave before she asks us to. It is so undignified
to wait until the lights are turned off." Sarah gathered her purse from the
floor, and panted with the exertion of bending down to retrieve it. "Why

is it that those damned interior schmucks can't design proper furniture for restaurants so that we wouldn't have to place our purses on the floor? They make a woman's purse to be the carrier of every known bacteria, because they expect it to heel like a well trained dog under the table on the dirty floor. Damn them. It was a nice lunch; see you at church on Sunday." And she was gone. Her three friends followed silently. Sarah could be so outspoken and even hostile.

THREE

During the drive home, Katharina could not free herself from the memory of the conversation at lunch. Like resin, the unpleasant thoughts stuck to her reflections and the more she tried to free herself, the stickier it became. She felt uneasy just about everything said, including the silent accusation that she was still not able to pick up the pieces of her life, and was not engaged in some meaningful activity.

Before her life path was shocked out of its established orbit she was a confirmed optimist; nothing could dim her positive outlook. However, her optimism was shattered along with so many other things, and uncharacteristically for her, negative words and allusions had a heretofore unknown power over her emotional life. Her friends meant well as they tried to prod her along, yet she was vexed. It took several miles of driving, when more out of a lifelong habit than conviction she set about to logically eliminate all disturbing thoughts, and to neutralize the observations made by her friends.

She shook her head impatiently. It was all so wrong. They looked into a distorted mirror and believed that the twisted view they saw in there was the absolute truth. But the mirror was damaged, and every one of her friends was mistaken. Or were they? Norms, regarded as right and even sacred, sometimes turn out to be the opposite of their assigned value; and wrongs at times appear to be less so. The path, which formerly appeared solid and straight, suddenly was no longer so: it was full of treacherous sandpits and led into dead ends. The railings, which were dependable and strong, built for support, suddenly gave way and there was nothing left to hang on. Everything was in flux, yet in order to go on living, the structure needed to be reinforced and made secure again.

Susan must be wrong in her belief about entering easier into a second marriage just because the first one was good. That was not all true, even though a dozen years ago Katharina too fell in love a second time, and after a fairly long courtship married again. But that was ten long years ago. Time, always marked by a special sort of relativity not even mentioned by Einstein, was flying much faster as she grew older, and age finally caught up with her. She became settled, almost timid. Changes were increasingly more frightening; only familiar faces and places were secure. The time of expectations and hope for great beginnings was over. She was progressively more suspicious and apprehensive about unknown territories. Adventures and the urge for new discoveries dwindled with the first signs of arthritis. She, a constant and experienced traveler during most of her life, became uneasy even during the short airplane flight she took to visit an ailing relative. With barely concealed panic she kept checking at regular intervals her ticket, the flight number, the gate, the time, her purse and handbag, and was baffled when she deplaned at the once familiar, but lately modernized airport, which bore little resemblance to the one she was used to. She hated to drive in a strange city, and felt uncomfortable when she had to take care of official business. What does Susan mean by going easily into a new situation or relation? She does not know what she is talking about. Besides, nobody could take Martin's place, no matter what Susan's neat little theory said about this issue. Once she talked about this to Susan, who listened carefully, and then remarked with the kind and careful consideration of a physician, who is about to announce a difficult, albeit not fatal diagnosis to worried relatives, "Katharina, your trouble is a careful heart."

And Lettie was wrong. One should not give up all memories, but keep them with reverence and gratitude, because only those can hold loneliness at bay. Lettie could and often did defend her withdrawal from the shrieking, cocktail–marinated, plastic–coated, superficial masses of the big city. She had a deep need for a tranquil island and craved truth and sincerity. She wanted nothing as much as to be left alone. "I'm not out to save the world," she had once confessed to Katharina with a small, apologetic smile. "I wouldn't even know how. I haven't the ambition of the Maid of Orleans. I am only concerned about the integrity of *my* home and *my* life. The important things I'm concerned about do not reach beyond the doorstep of my house. Secretly I think that the world would be better off if we all did just that, or at least that much. Leave the great deeds to Joan and her kind. The rest of us should clean out our own house first, and the world would be a nicer and safer place. In my case this starts with downsizing and simplifying." Sarah, if she were present, would have grunted some dissenting response, because her own actions were directed toward saving the world, while her personal life was unsatisfactory. She was intelligent enough to realize this, and Lettie's remarks would have touched a vulnerable point, and made her grunt deeper and more painful. Katharina, of course, had her own doubts about the issue. Lettie's philosophy had its appeal, but the practice of it, as is usually the case, was far more difficult, if not impossible. One does not simply close up a segment of life in the manner one closes a weekend house at the end of the season. Katharina could not build a future without a past, of that she was certain. Yes, Lettie had a point, but is it possible to accept and to implement it? There were always men who renounced the uncertain world and went out into the wilderness to commune with God, or with their own inner self. But it is not a pastime designed for everybody. Lettie found a happy mean between the wilderness and the city, but of course, she has her art, and it is a mighty crutch.

And finally Sarah too was wrong, even more wrong than the other two friends. Her negative outlook was damaged and damaging. She was forever dismayed and unhappy with life, with people, with everything she encountered. That surely was a brutal error. Noble or inspiring things did not exist as far as she could see, and through the fog of her chronic maladjustment the world appeared cursed with incurable maladies and the people in it were mostly worthless. Her fine mind and good heart were poisoned with self–destructing irony and touched with vulgarity. Katharina suspected that she used both to cover up some hurts, which she chose never to mention. But it was true that at the same time she neglected to learn the fine art of suffering fools gladly, nor had she any intentions of learning it at this late date. She could not see that the world was both beautiful and awful, that there is birth as well as death, joy and pain, sickness and health, light and shadow; the list is endless. She could not see that because of its very imperfection the world is perfect, and it has to be accepted as such. She was unable to enjoy the precious time given to her, which is hardly more than a moment in the cosmic timetable, a gift to mankind between birth and eternity. Sarah closed her eyes and also her soul to the world. She has not noticed a sunrise in years; she turned her back on most everything the world has to offer. It is unhealthy to live with bitterness for years, and somehow it is not consistent with her eagerness to do good works. Her words and actions are not in harmony. One or the other must be fake, and she is fatally caught in the restless disquiet of her soul.

Katharina caught herself for a moment. She was mouthing platitudes in which she no longer believed. Her life was arid, and she could barely force herself to live from one day to the next without breaking down. The beauty and the wholeness of the world was no more than a worn cliché anymore, and she had no business praising it. There was a time she believed in all that goodness and beauty, but now the statements were not born of unshakable conviction, and so she strayed into the shallows of banality. But she chased the thought from her mind and added stubbornly: I will get well again, and then the world will be a friendly place once more, and I will again love its grandeur.

After Katharina so carefully dismissed all sticky thoughts that did not fit into her way of seeing things, she was a little more relaxed, almost at peace.

Before she unlocked the front door, out of habit she pulled the handful of mail from the box. Most of it was addressed to the resident or to the boxholder. The world has shrunk. The amount, the content and the quality of the daily mail was a fairly accurate indicator of what life was all about, and how much she counted for others. Martin, after opening his stack of get–well cards, remarked once, "My friends are letting me know that the end is very much in sight, and there is no hope left for me."

"What makes you think so?" Katharina was horrified.

"Very simple. In the beginning I used to get loads of funny cards. Each was worth a belly laugh about gorgeous nurses, breakfasts served in bed, the Ritz–treatment, and so on. Lately my cards are strongly religious, packed with prayers and sympathy. Death is relentlessly approaching, and it is no joking matter. No one dares to make fun of it. Our friends are getting ready for the solemn occasion with a lot of prefabricated sanctimonious fluff. Friends, who can recite the entire Gettysburg Address, but are stuck after the first six words of the Lord's Prayer, assure me of their spiritual support and send me their prayers. Whom are they kidding?"

Sympathy cards followed the get–well cards, and then even that stopped, and she was reduced to 'resident', who could be induced to buy something useless at a special price.

She dropped her keys on the Chippendale table in the entrance hall, and stopped to listen to the silence for a moment. It was Rosie's day off. The house was magnificent and terribly empty; the great arena of her loneliness promised yet another evening void of any sort of meaning. The soul had departed. She thought she could hear her own heart beat. It took some effort to move on from the entrance. As soon as she put her coat away, the phone was ringing.

"Grandmother? This is Karen. I need your wisdom and calm and also your hug. Can I come over?"

"Of course, you can. Drive carefully; the roads are slick from the rain. And I love you."

"I love you too."

Katharina was disturbed. One more emotional encounter would be too much on this rainy, cold day. However, when Karen arrived, she was far from the distraught young woman her phone call seemed to indicate. Dressed smartly in beige pants and a mohair turtleneck of the same color, she walked into her grandmother's living room, tall and self–assured.

"Hi Granny, you look good. I wanted to visit you, because our house is so desperately empty. Laura is growing roots in the library at the university, and mom's late hours match those of dad's. My former friends are either happily married, cooing over babies, or pursuing fantastic careers. I don't belong anywhere. All I can show is my divorce papers."

"Good of you to come and visit. Tea or coffee? If you give me a few minutes, I'll whip up a wonderful bread pudding for us. Nowadays I don't keep any goodies handy in the house."

"Tea, please, and I want to watch the making of the pudding more than I want to eat it."

"That would be a mistake, because it is really delicious. And the virtue of the pudding is that it can be on the table in no time at all. Come to the kitchen."

Katharina put the kettle of water for tea on the stove, then chopped up some left–over biscuits, gingersnaps, and mixed it with beaten eggs, melted butter, cream, milk, some crumbled marzipan, rum, and sliced almonds. She let it stand while she put her favorite Herend tea service on a tray. Karen sat at the breakfast counter, where Martin used to sit, and examined the birds on the teacups.

"Very pretty. But why do the birds have a necklace in their beaks?"

"Some old, romantic story, I forgot what it is exactly. The jewel of a famous lady, perhaps the Baroness Rothschield, was lost and the birds found it, or stole it, I can't recall which."

"Imagine a thing being immortalized on an expensive tea service for having been lost! I lose things all the time and nobody really cares, nor designs a tea service in memory of it… Whatever made you prepare bread pudding for the first time?" Karen's keen, but undisciplined mind could not stay long with any one topic. Her thoughts flitted from one thing to the next and did not stay long anywhere. "It really sounds gross. I know it isn't, because I know how well you cook and bake, but its name does not sound very appetizing, does it? For some reason it brings to mind a cup of soaked and swollen bread, a soggy pulp and no bite to it. It doesn't sound appealing."

"No, it doesn't. But that is merely prejudice, and you can shortchange yourself if you judge something sight unseen, like I did in Germany."

"Granny! I can't believe it! You were actually prejudiced?"

"And how! Your grandfather and I toured that country for several weeks during a hot summer. We did everything conscientiously, like professional tourists should. We sampled most of the native food, with the exception of one. *Rote Grütze* kept appearing on the menu in several restaurants, but it sounded as gross as bread pudding. We thought '*Grütze*' was grits. Anyway, it sounded like it. You know, like hominy. I do not know too many people, who are crazy about hominy for dessert, although I might be wrong. And then this *Grütze* thing was supposed to be red. Red hominy! No thank you, I don't think so. However, on our last night we were daring, and bravely ordered this culinary wonder. Needless to say, it was delicious, and it had nothing to do with grits."

"What was it?"

"A great variety of berries probably cooked in red wine, then mixed into gelatin, and all of it covered with whipped cream. It was heavenly. I never found the recipe for it, and when I tried to reconstruct, I failed miserably. All I got was berries in red gelatin, not even close to this *Rote Grütze*. So much for prejudice based on ignorance."

"Aren't all prejudices based on ignorance?"

"Right. And this deadly mixture is the most dangerous threat to the world." Katharina turned to Karen with a smile. "I was thinking about something along this same line before you came; I mean about closed minds and prejudice. What would you think of a woman in her sixties, who would want to marry again?"

"Grandmother! Not you?" Karen was not even trying to hide her shock.

"Of course not. It was just an academic question."

"Oh. Well, I guess it is all right. I suppose it's really awful for some people to live alone. They have a right to arrange their life as they wish. We don't get shocked seeing old married people together, I mean those, who got old together. Some of them are rather cute when they are holding hands and care for each other. But it is hard to imagine that two oldsters would start, you know..."

"Yes I do know," she said quietly, and the indication did not escape her that it might be all right for other people to do so, but it would be shocking if such an event would hit close to home. Poor Susan. Her children probably branded her and the new partner as dirty old people, just a little this side of being public dangers and menaces to the cherished, but petrified morality of society. Didn't well–meaning people still run some retirement homes as if they were monasteries and nunneries? According to this unwritten law, or crazy expectation, Susan's role was to be that of a dignified widow, a quasi–virgin in conservative dresses and no desires. She had no business turning against conventions.

Katharina spooned the mixture into buttered ramekins and shoved them into the oven.

"Fifteen minutes will do. I have no whipping cream, but vanilla ice cream will go fine with it. And how are you nowadays?"

"Fine. The worst is over. It was a mistake to marry what's–his–name. If I was foolish enough to do so, I should have left him sooner. Like immediately after the ceremony. Good riddance. Now I can start living my life."

"How?"

"I want to go back to school for graduate work. Mom and Dad offered financial help, but I'd hate to accept it. I plan to finance my continuing education personally. I have some money of my own, but plan to work until next fall to add to my savings."

"Doing what?"

"Waiting tables. I started yesterday. Not actually working, but sort of training for it. At the Country Club. The girl who recommended me there says that she makes really good money, and the guests are definitely better than your basic crowd in a hamburger joint, and they tip well for good service. The hours aren't too bad either, unless there is a special occasion, like a wedding or an anniversary party. No drunks and no fanny–pinchers. After I have enough money, I'll do grad school full time. It does not take all that long; besides, I love school. It should be a piece of cake. When it is all over, I'll wait tables again for a while to make enough money so I can do the knapsack tour of Europe."

"Your life is all planned out perfectly," Katharina said.

"Indeed, but it is no guarantee that I won't fall on my face again. Remember the radiant bride of a little while ago, who was at the top of the world? Those were truly great expectations, but they exploded before I learned how to sign my new name. And then there I was with my face in the mud."

"Not all expectations are doomed to fail. This time you'll make it fine."

Katharina served the bread pudding, poured more tea and looked with pleasure at her granddaughter. Karen had enormous hazel eyes, which dominated her face and beamed at the world with youthful, innocent joy. She captivated everyone with that sincere look and easy laugh. Curiously the divorce did not mark her face with bitterness, and she seemed to regard it not as an unfortunate end, but as the beginning of something new and wonderful. One must be born with the right set of genes, or be young all over again, to survive a crash this splendidly, Katharina concluded.

"This bread pudding is delicious! You are a lady of many talents, but it is obvious that you were born to cook," Karen complimented.

"Just call me Emeril. Or Bocuse, if you want to show a little Continental savvy."

"I envy you, Grandma. I can't cook. Once I tried to bake a cake for what's–his–name's birthday and he congratulated me on my expertise in geology."

"Geology?"

"Yeah. He said I achieved a dubious first in the culinary arts for creating a stone cake. For some reason it refused to rise, and had the consistency of granite, more or less. A stone cake, unlike the stone soup of our childhood's storybooks, has no moral at all. I should have served it on his head, then scratched on his tombstone, 'Here lies a piece of cake'. Or save some money on the engraving and just write, 'Here lies a piece.'"

"Did he often belittle you?"

"Let's put it this way: if I were a thousand–year old *sequoia gigantea*, he would have whittled me down during the year of our marriage so much that what remained could not have yielded enough to make a toothpick."

"Why did he do it?" Katharine asked, as if an answer were possible. At the same time she had to control a smile, wanting to spread over her face. Karen was going to be like her mother. Young as she was, she already knew how to make fun of life's lousy turns.

"Because he was a merciless sonofabitch of no consequence. He cannot help what he is; he is a rare case study. A psychologist could earn a Ph.D. by just writing him up. The fault was mine for not seeing it before the church bells started ringing. But of course, his one outstanding talent was the art of acting. He could fool you into believing anything he wanted you to believe, including the illusion of his perfection and devotion."

There was no comment to this, so Katharina asked in a soothing voice, "Surely he had some good points too? Everybody has them."

Karen was dwelling on the question for a little while, and then said, "Here you go again Granny, trying to find goodness in everybody, including prehistoric animals. But you are right; he did have good points. Several as a matter of fact. For example he could, anywhere, at any time of the day or night, tell you without the help of a clock or watch exactly what time it is. It was really uncanny, because he was never off more than 5 or 10 minutes, which is par for the course. Mom's grandfather clock does the same, but we are not about to throw it out because of it. He was also extremely pleasant at all times to salesclerks, waiters and door–to–door salesmen, and talked tenderly to my goldfish. He dressed well, was very good looking, and was always the life of any party. He also won every argument, mostly because at the end I usually gave up talking to the walls. I soon found out that these virtues were not enough for marital bliss."

After a moment of reflective pause Karen took a second helping of the pudding, then as was her way, asked unexpectedly,"Are you sorry that you gave up practicing?"

The question hung in the air for a short while, and there was no ready answer for it.

"Probably not," Katharina finally answered. "I did it for almost four decades and it filled my life. But there is a point in everybody's life when work becomes labor, and dedication becomes difficult and tiresome. This is the time to stop and leave. And our life with Martin was so rich and rewarding that there was never any vacuum. Now that he is gone, work could perhaps fill the void, but I am too old, and have been out of it for too long."

"It has not been all that long, Grandmother!"

"The way medicine is forging ahead, I consider my absence from it too long. Too many improvements happened since, of which I know nothing. Patients deserve a doctor who is on top of things and who knows the newest discoveries and methods. Karen, my darling, I am also getting old. I once heard about a colleague, who insisted to work long past her eightieth birthday. People adored her and thought she was great, even though at times she would give a shot through her patient's pantyhose. That is not for me."

While Karen chuckled over this, Katharina removed the plates and poured more tea. Karen's remark touched a nerve, and she needed time to think about it. As the initial pain after the funeral became more bearable, Katharina increasingly found herself out of sorts. Used to a very active life, suddenly she had nothing to do. Formerly it was her conviction that to a great extent work defines the person, but during the years with Martin she forgot about this, and did not miss work at all. Now that she was alone and had no important work to do, she felt diminished and lost. Her days were spent wandering aimlessly in the large house, doing meaningless little tasks, reading, and sometimes doing errands. She was bored, disoriented, circling in a holding pattern, waiting for death to give the signal. Karen knew what she was talking about.

"I always lived with two mortal fears," Katharina finally said. "One was that somehow, someday I would cause death while driving my car. The other was, that due to some unforgivable mistake or misdiagnosis I would kill one of my patients. Both happens, you know. As I am turning old I'm increasingly afraid of both. I am starting to dislike driving, and I don't want to practice again."

"Are you serious?"

"Absolutely. After I received my diploma, a former roommate with an excessively sharp tongue and a degree in art–history gave me an engraved plate, which hung for a long time above my desk at the home I shared with your grandfather. Perhaps you recall seeing it."

"What did it say?"

"A quotation from the Bible: '*And Nathan, being sick, trusted not the Lord, but sent for a physician —and Nathan was gathered into his fathers'.*'"

"Very funny and cruel."

"Not really. It kept me in line and made me humble and very, very careful."

"You could attend some refresher seminar or something. We could go to school together."

"And make some sort of a record?"

"Why not? Or you could take classes with Laura and share a meaningful friendship with some exotic bacteria. There are so many of them, and some are very, very lonely and in need of good company."

"Surely, you jest!" Katharina laughed with the old, happy abandon. "Friendship with an exotic bacteria? Then you don't know Laura or me! We both are sworn enemies of those things, and only have murder in our hearts when we meet them."

"OK. A meaningful affair, enriched with lots of quality time is out with those microscopic monsters. But still, Granny, I think that soon you will be hankering for something to do. Being active in some medicine–related field is better than learning to do needlepoint. My grandmother is not the woman, who was made to live out the rest of her life in dead time."

Katharina smiled at Karen, and patted her hand.

"You are wonderful," she said simply, but added silently, 'it is wonderful to be young and unwithered, to look forward without fear, and to anticipate life and all its promises. But it is even more wonderful to have a grand-daughter, who is willing to reach out and help an old lady take the path with her.'

"In other words, you are going to consider it?"

"I will think about it," she promised.

"Is it the same thing? I mean to consider, or to think about it?"

"Almost. Almost, my love."

FOUR

For a day or two disquieting thoughts overwhelmed Katharina. Alexa's e-mail worried her, Karen's great disappointment, despite the cheerful front she put up to cover it, hurt her, and Susan's impending marriage gave rise to mostly undefined, uneasy emotions. But most of all she was thinking about Karen's suggestion of engaging herself in a meaningful activity. 'The mind is willing, but body and spirit object,' was the way Martin put it, when he faced a task he would rather not do. Katharina felt the same way. She knew that she should somehow put herself in gear and become active once again, but totally lacked the energy and enthusiasm for it.

Rosie was polishing something somewhere in the house, although since Martin was gone the place lost its lived-in look. Cooking was absolutely minimal, social life was non-existent, and Rosie was gradually repeating herself by polishing the same polished silver and dusting the same dustless shelves. But Katharina kept her, not only because she disliked housework, but because it felt good to have another human being in the house during the day.

She was done with her daily ritual of caring for the houseplants, and wandered into the gleaming, unused kitchen. The days of great dinner parties were gone, and her modest meals did not require this kitchen, which could pass as the feeding center of a medium sized hotel. She looked at the shelves, packed with dishes, bowls, platters, kept ever ready by Rosie. The small built-in desk tucked away in the corner and complete with a telephone was her planning center for her parties.

Absentmindedly she reached for the file on the shelf. It was her policy never to serve the same meal twice to guests, and to avoid repetitions, she always wrote the list of invited guests for each dinner party, and jotted down the menu served. She noted the rough schedule, which Rosie called the 'count-down', needed for the preparation, and underlined items, which were hard to get, or had to be ordered for the menu. There were occasional remarks about table decorations, drinks, comments the guests made about the meal, and she even noted the dress she wore.

She flipped the cards with something close to disbelief. Was she really this concerned about silly details? All that seemed so terribly trivial in retrospect. And yet, was not this very devotion to every tiny detail, which made her parties so extraordinary? And was Martin not always so very pleased with the success of an evening? He loved dinner parties, and never failed to thank her after the guests left. His praise was lavish and sincere. No, she decided, it was not at all trivial, because a perfect party was strangely important to Martin, and what was important to Martin, was never unimportant to her. He was always exuberant when guests overwhelmed them with compliments. Once, after everyone left, he tried to explain in rather vague terms his views about it. He said that the lifestyle they showed to the world confirmed their personal values; the perfection of the dinner table was one of their hallmarks. But Katharina was exhausted from said perfect party and was too tired to listen to his philosophy. She smiled her wifely smile at him, kissed him gently and drifted off to the bedroom. Now standing in the kitchen she knew that whatever made him this happy could not have been trivial, and if she could start all over, she would do it exactly this way again.

"Are you planning a dinner party?" Rosie asked surprised. She came so silently that Katharina almost dropped the file, as she did not hear her entering the kitchen. "Didn't mean to startle you," she apologized, "Just thought you were planning something, because you are looking at your files."

"I might have my friends over to celebrate an approaching wedding," she answered, and then wondered why she said it, since a minute ago this plan did not even enter her head. Rosie removed her most trusted cleaning agent, a bottle of vinegar from the shelf, and then left again, but with a small smile. The gloom of the once vibrant household depressed her, and the party coming up gave her hope that the dismal mourning period is perhaps over. Katharina was still standing with the box of cards in her hand, and then she knew that indeed, she wanted to invite her friends.

"It won't be a traditional bridal shower," she told Lettie, the first one she called. "I want a little get–together to celebrate Susan's new life, and to give her our gifts. She won't have a wedding, or a reception in the traditional sense, so we might as well do something on our own, just the four of us, and Alexa. I wouldn't dream of including her family. I'm afraid, even if they accepted they would make everybody feel uncomfortable. I want this to be a happy occasion."

And so it happened that for the first time in almost a year Katharina immersed herself into the preparation of a gourmet dinner, once again paying close attention to every little detail. The color of the flowers she ordered complemented perfectly the hues of the china; the silver and crystals gleamed, like in the old days. The candles and the fireplace were lit, and the food turned out as expected; the months while Katharina did not cook anything noteworthy did not diminish her skills.

The ladies, even Lettie, wore formal dresses, but Alexa was the most magnificent in her simple, formfitting gown, triple–strand pearl necklace, smooth hair and ripe womanhood. Katharina did not compliment her, but stood back and silently admired this perfection of feminine beauty. Sarah stood close and noticed the expression on Katharina's face.

"Don't Kathy! Don't fall into the same trap Niobe built for herself. Latona was overreacting to be sure, and without doubt she was a world class bitch. Nonetheless, gods are merciless, and you know it. They hate comparisons, especially with mortals, and are violently allergic to one–upmanship. Better be careful, lest you too will learn to weep like a stone."

"I didn't know you were superstitious."

"Then you don't know me."

"Thanks for the warning," Katharina laughed at her friend. "I'll keep it in mind. Meanwhile let me feast my eyes on her, and allow me the arrogance of saying that if I had not done anything else in my life but have her, it was worth to be born. I hope this joy does not make me into a presumptuous mortal, lacking in humility and deserving Olympian punishment."

"Not in my eyes; however, the upper crust on the Cynthian Mountain might see things differently. They have issues of their own."

Katharina, shrugging her shoulders, smiled, and whispered into Sarah's ears the lines of W.S. Landor:

> *'may not a mother in her pride repeat*
> *what every mortal said?'*

Sarah laughed too, "It is a good thing mothers aren't partial. Or at least not much." Alexa, perhaps sensing that they were talking about her, sauntered across the room and joined them.

"I think you were born in the wrong century and in the wrong country," Sarah told her in a voice that carried and caught the attention of the others."Your beauty should have been displayed at royal courts, where it would have been enjoyed like a piece of art by connoisseurs, and celebrated by kings and princes." She then turned to Katharina and added *sotto voce* and with an impish smile, "I'm not her mother, so I may praise her without the classical consequences which Niobe had to suffer."

"Sarah is right for once," commented Lettie. "I would love to paint you, although portraits are not really my thing. But I feel I could do you. I can see you as a queen on the canvas: aloof and self–assured in the knowledge that your elegant bones are perfect and your colors just right, your power unquestionable. Cool and magnificent, feminine and majestic but burning inside with a mighty, sacred fire of sensual and spiritual passion. It is a perfect and dramatic combination. I would concentrate on your unbelievably gorgeous eyes."

"You both embarrass me," Alexa protested. "However, next time when I'll be deeply immersed in scrubbing the toilets, I'll remember your remarks. It will help me through the ordeal as I choke in the thick cloud of ammonia gas to know that I'm really an exiled queen, and somebody will eventually hang for making me remove urine stains from the tile."

"Do that. But think about it: I was serious in wanting to do your portrait. And never use detergents with chlorine in the bathroom. Ammonia on the floor, which is a given with a man in the house, combined with chlorine in the cleaning fluid is a deadly combination."

"I don't know what to say to your offer, Lettie. I mean about the portrait, not the chlorine. It sounds like such a strange experience. Sort of old–fashioned and aristocratic."

"Not any stranger than having your picture taken at a photo studio. Only this takes longer, and in the end you don't have the choice between several proofs to choose the best. What I paint is what you get. But remember, a painter does not imitate; she puts on her canvas the essence, at least as she sees it. Get it? My paintbrush is not like the lens of a camera – it goes much deeper, all the way to the core of you. If I interpreted you correctly, you'll agree with my work and perhaps will even love the portrait; if I was mistaken, and my idea of you is not the same as your idea about yourself, you will hate it."

"Do you allow for personal biases?" Sarah asked, but Lettie did not answer. She was never certain whether Sarah was seriously wicked, or wickedly funny.

"Thanks, Lettie, your offer honors me. I'll think about it, and meanwhile I'll try to get used to the idea."

Katharina served the cocktails, and the usual small, happy talk followed. Women, when in each other's company, usually have a good time. At such times they are not concerned with the burning questions of the universe, and are not trying to solve economic problems, or to save the world from its assortment of ills. This is not due to lack of brains or interest, but they simply follow the unwritten and generally accepted law, which states that these get–togethers are for relaxation, recreation, laughter, friendship and general well being. The nagging issues are left on the hooks with the overcoats in the entrance hall. The time is used to reestablish connections while affection and care for each other flow freely. Women do not attempt to whip up the adrenalin and blood pressure to unhealthy levels with politics and social issues they can't solve anyhow, but which are sure to raise the stress level and so ruin the evening.

"What a table," Susan exclaimed later as they walked into the dining room. "I'm glad George isn't here, lest he would get ideas and expect such style in our home, when I'll be serving macaroni and cheese for supper."

"We didn't eat like this every day, Susan. Most people, who have to suffer their way through life without cooks and butlers, don't. But if you need to put up a dog and pony show once in a while for some V.I.P. or for a very special occasion, it is not all that difficult," said Katharina. "Each year it takes a bit more time, and your physical recovery period usually stretches for several days after the event, but it can be done. Fortunately though, as we grow older we have less and less reasons to have to impress somebody."

She poured the wine after the oysters, which even Sarah enjoyed. According to her personal vegetarian creed she would not eat anything that had a face. She decided that oysters do not have one.

There was a little pause before the main course was served, and Sarah in her usual straightforward way asked without any preliminaries, "Susan, did your family accept your decision by now, or are you still in the doghouse?"

"I don't know, and with each passing day I care less. I still visit them as before on account of the grandchildren, but the 'problem' as they call our impending marriage, is not being mentioned. I am so worn out by their collective schizophrenia that I can hardly wait to leave it all behind."

"And so, all here assembled, witness ye the workings of yet another model family." The cynical remark, of course, came from Sarah.

"We are sailing in less than two weeks, but they made it into a non–event," Susan continued with a shrug. " 'If we don't acknowledge it, it is not there', is the way they deal with it. The white elephant is sitting on the pink couch in the living room, but nobody sees it. And when they sweep it under the carpet, nobody mentions that strange hump under the rug. And the closer the date of our departure, the less important is to me what the family will do with that white elephant."

"That a girl," commented Sarah. "Don't get too hung up on this wretched sense of family obligation, or similar noble and nebulous sentiments. In the end, when things will get bad,—and trust me, things will get extraordinarily bad,—you can only rely on yourself, on your walker, your Medicare and if you are really lucky and have a partner, who is a tad stronger than you are, then on him. Forget the rest of the loving relatives. They don't care, and will poop on your head from high above. Better forget about them, but in any case, have a sturdy umbrella handy. It will prevent that unmentionables, courtesy of family, drop straight on your head."

Alexa glanced at her mother, but refrained from making a comment, which was not needed anyhow. Verbal communication was not always needed between them. After the guests would leave, or the following day, they could discuss what was said and reassure each other. Generalizations did not apply to their relationship and at any rate Sarah's bitterness was spoken in a language foreign to them, and her negative views did not make any sense in their world.

"Wars, whether fought among nations, religions, or families, usually are devastating but ultimately pointless," Katharina said. The women looked at her with puzzled expression, because her statement seemed incongruous. Seeing the perplexed faces, she tried to explain her proposal. "To clarify my point, think about the last big war, and you'll get the most disturbing picture, and you'll understand the connection. Think of the four powers fighting Germany and Japan. Their sacred alliance was indelibly etched on our memory with that memorable outdoor photo of the four leaders sitting in a row in Yalta, like fat cats digesting a good meal. This event was shortly followed by the gigantic effort, fueled by the Marshall Plan, to rebuild Germany, which was almost totally destroyed by their combined and eminent air forces during the war. At this point of frenzied rebuilding our attention was momentarily diverted by princess Elizabeth Alexandra Mary giving birth to a son, who would perhaps be the heir one day to the British throne, and a playmate to Camilla, and we kept our fingers crossed during the Berlin Airlift. So occupied, we hardly noticed that meanwhile the Cold War raging between the former friends, was escalating into a situation, which could have set the world on fire once again. Now the former friends passionately hated each other. Each deployed tens of thousands of troops at strategic locations, never mind the lethal weapons that went with it. To pass away time, each commenced to court the former enemies. The world was just getting used to this new constellation, when behold, the enemies made friends once more, successfully destroyed the Berlin Wall, and were trying to figure out meanwhile whom to hate next. You practically have to read the daily paper to see whether you are expected to trust or mistrust a current power. And this has been repeated all through history."

"And your point is?" asked Sarah. She was known at times to detour in her own conversation, but did not tolerate this weakness in others. But Katharina, once in gear to explain an idea, did not let herself be easily discouraged, and continued to talk.

"Families too get hurt, fight, break ties, and then spend years patching it all up."

"Like Susan's family," interjected Lettie.

"Hers, and millions of others. So much wasted energy and effort! So much fire, brimstone, atomic threat and hurt feelings, while the world, ideologies and families change their unprincipled mind constantly. Some call it sticking to moral principles, others diplomacy, and still others defend it saying that it all started, when he hit back. Mix in a little greed, jealousy and pride, (often false pride) and you have the makings of an evil brew. But it takes just a little time, even historically speaking, and then everybody is back again at square one. One wonders, why all the fire and smoke was necessary, when things could get back on their own to where they were to begin with. If only each newly wrought alliance or ideology would not come too late for too many! Basing my opinion on this knowledge, I'm sure Susan, that your family will come around sooner or later, and will accept your decision. Peace will be restored, as if all this never happened."

"May you have spoken in the tongue of angels, who according to rumors know many more answers than we do," the bride answered.

"And may it happen rather sooner than later," Sarah concluded. "And Kathy, you may now get off your soapbox, please." She did, and continued to serve her elaborate meal.

After the main course, Katharina served in dainty dishes a chocolate dessert, topped with whipping cream and a maraschino cherry. Sarah examined the tiny portions with critical eyes.

"Kathy, you are really trying to look out for my expanding ass, which is soon to be about the size of Montana going east to west. You should have served this in a thimble. What is it anyhow?"

"*Pots–au–chocolat*. Very rich, very old–fashioned, and very aristocratic. It was often served at the Viennese imperial court, and you would not be able to eat more of it than what I am serving."

"In other words, you are trying to educate us to be familiar with the better things in life, while watching over our girth."

"Just wanted to spoil you little," Katharina said and when the little pots were empty, and nobody wanted more coffee, she ushered her guests into the living room to open the presents.

"We discussed at great length what to give you, Susan," she announced. "Since in a very short while you are going to combine two richly furnished homes into one, your priority ought to be a garage sale; you do not need more debris added to a house already bursting at its seems. So our gifts will not burden you with useless things. What we are giving you is strictly hedonistic, to make your life extravagantly pampered, and as you use them they'll disappear, leaving only the wrappings behind."

They sat in a semicircle in front of the fireplace and Katharina filled their glasses.

"I was debating between a wheelchair and an electric blanket, but decided on something else," Sarah said pointing to a large box. "At your age you should practice safe eating, which means avoiding food, if you know what I mean. I chose my gift with that in mind."

There was laughter as Susan ripped off the wrapping to reveal a case of fine champagne.

Lettie's equally large box contained a great variety of candles, some scented or floating, others tapered or formed into intricate sculptures in subdued, elegant colors. "Romance is not the sole privilege of youth," she said quietly. "Why waste a good thing on kids, who already have so much of everything else?"

Alexa selected bath salts, some from the Dead Sea; also oils, fine soaps, body powders and lotions.

Katharina's gift came in an envelope: a coupon to the city's finest spa.

"They'll make you glow for your wedding," Katharina assured Susan. "They offer a complete line of pampering from body massage to a facial. You'll feel great and years younger, although God knows, you don't seem to need it."

"Now I finally feel like a bride, rather than a social misfit, recommended for extensive therapy," Susan said amidst a lot of laughter. There was a moment of awkward silence, as the disapproval of the bride's family became almost palpable in Katharina's living room. This was such a pleasant evening, and was so easily arranged. Why could her family not accept her decision and offer such a celebration? They were withholding their blessing and refused to share in the joy. This was cruel and sad. Susan deserved better, but then we don't all get what we deserve.

It was Sarah again, who bridged the silence.

"Life is full of frustrations and challenges, but despite every lousy and creaky start in the morning, eventually you'll find your dentures, your bifocals and your walker, and nothing can stop you from starting each day with a bang. The hell with everybody else. You have no other concern now, but each other. Forget the poop, which others attempt to dish out for you. We all wish you happiness. People usually have the crude habit of adding, 'and a long life', but I'm more careful. I only wish unparalleled quality in your life, never mind, how long or how short."

After her guests left and Katharina packed away the leftovers and loaded the dishwasher, she sat for a long time in her favorite chair near the fireplace. She recalled Susan at her husband's funeral.

His was the first death in their group and it touched them all deeply. Susan's grief was shattering. She stood at the grave, supported by her children, and held a handkerchief in front of her face during the entire ritual. It is strange, how in moments of deeply felt grief a few inconsequential details stand out and get stuck in memory. Katharina never forgot Susan's unusual handkerchief, the square of stark whiteness bordered in black. She has never seen anything like it before, but its similarity to the black border on the announcement of her husband's death made it even more poignant.

Once, still in elementary school, Katharina was caught passing notes to her friends. As a punishment her fifth grade teacher ordered her to memorize three poems. She completely forgot two of them, and from the third, the Woodspurge, by Dante Gabriel Rossetti, she could only remember four lines:

> *From perfect grief there need not be*
> *Wisdom, or even memory:*
> *One thing then learnt remains to me,–*
> *The woodspurge has a cup of three.*

Just as Rossetti could not perceive anything else in his perfect grief but the three petals of the humble flower on which his gaze was riveted; so for Katharina that handkerchief was the only reality during the funeral. The black–edged batiste was to her what the trillium was to Rossetti.

After they left the cemetery they were convinced that this pain would never go away. And yet, today Susan was happy and beautiful, looking forward to a shared life, which might not last all that long. She certainly must be aware of this, yet is so happy that this black cloud gathering at the horizon cannot extinguish her joy.

Katharina had no marital plans, but she wondered whether there would ever be a time, when she too would laugh happily once again, like Susan did today. It was a barely expressed dream–wish to be carefree and joyful again, or at least not be so broken up.

She wanted to believe that Susan's obvious happiness was a promise that pain, just like happiness and time, would also be transitory. She sighed and knew that even if it was a definite promise, the time for it did not yet arrive.

⊛ Sunset

FIVE

It was a dismal Saturday morning. Katharina sat in the kitchen, still in her robe and slippers, having a third cup of coffee. She was infinitely tired and listless and saw no reason to get dressed, or do anything. It was a morning of acute backsliding. A few days ago she felt her energies resurging, and actually enjoyed preparing the dinner for her friends, but today was another day, and she missed Martin so keenly that she had to leave the kitchen. She could not bear seeing the empty chair where he once sat. Finally the insistent ringing of the phone moved her out of that deadly immobility.

"Good morning, Grandma, it is me, Laura. I was wondering if you would come shopping with me? I decided that this year I'll do my holiday shopping very early, especially since after an hour of it, even without the Christmas throng, I am ready for the straight jacket and the padded cell. I hate to shop, it makes me ill, and I'll probably die of it. It would help to have a doctor at my side, when the worst happens. Please."

"I…"

"Wonderful. I'll drop off Mom at the airport and will pick you up after, that is an hour and a half from now. We can have lunch after the ordeal."

It was not such an ordeal after all. Laura, well organized as always, had a shopping list, knew exactly what she wanted and did not linger at every counter the way Alexa and Karen always did. As she went, she checked off the items, and when the number of her packages increased, she'd run out to the parking lot to deposit them in the trunk, while Katharina waited for her. She only hesitated when she had to select an item for her father.

"Why is it so hard to buy a gift for a man? I can find great things for twenty women in half an hour, but it takes weeks of consideration and aborted ideas until I find something suitable that could give him pleasure. Why?"

"For one thing my dear, men are so conservative that items for their wardrobe is out. They won't put on anything new until the day when that old, favorite sweater self–destructs."

"Which is not true of women."

"Not at all. One can find dozens of item in every price range for a woman to hang on herself and she'll be pleased with it. Second, it is an established no–no to buy him anything that would then belong to the house. You can buy house–gifts for a woman, and she'll love you for it – candles, pillows, objects of art, fancy tablecloths, name it. Don't even try the same line on men. I don't understand why this is so, but can you see your father's face if you'd buy him a toaster, or a tea service?" They both laughed at the idea. "Men also don't have many hobbies or diversions and those they have are excessively expensive. You can't really afford to buy an antic car, a golf cart, or things like that. Mostly they don't wear jewelry, and most shirts no longer require cuff links. A gift of theater or concert tickets are a waste for the men I know, including your father. And of course, this is where the root of the trouble lies buried."

"So we are back to ties and after shave lotions."

"Or sweaters."

"Of which he has as many as the number of Christmases in his adult life, multiplied by the number of women who buy gifts for him," Laura said. "Also, you already pointed out that he would probably not even wear any of it. I must think about this some more. Would he enjoy some exquisite wine, or does that count as a house–gift? Nevertheless, it has been a fruitful morning. I did everything, except his and yours. His, because I don't know what to get him, and yours, because it will be a surprise, and you are not supposed to be there when I buy that tea service or toaster you just mentioned. Ready for lunch?"

"My treat," said Katharina. The inertia and sadness of the morning vanished, and she walked with the old spring in her steps. As a matter of fact, instead of wanting to collapse around noon as she expected, she felt a new pleasure as they entered the restaurant.

"I am not much for a pre–lunch cocktail, but would enjoy a glass of wine with the meal, how about you?" she asked her granddaughter.

"Absolutely. I love the wine card. Even if I don't plan to have anything but seltzer, I always ask for it, because I love to read the descriptions, don't you, Grandma?" Laura said as she opened the wine card. "Listen to this: vibrant and soft, mature and silky. It could refer to a lovely and interesting middle–aged woman, who hasn't lost it yet, but is tempered with ripe feminine charm. And this one here is seductive with a floral nose… And this Chardonnay has a bold but elegant style with a depth and complexity. Please tell me about the complexity of a wine! What strange tales does it tell its shrink?" Laura giggled as she went on studying the wine list. "This one delivers a grassy simplicity, and the Sauvignon Blanc is lighthearted and capricious, the Merlot is innocently sensual and witty. I'd love to hear some of its sexy jokes… This one is displaying a renaissance flair, a well–rounded perfection. Now really!" Laura laughed again. "I suppose the grapes from which it was made spoke several languages, were well versed in the arts, understood the quantum theory, and made some discoveries in chemistry. Or did it acquire its universal education in the oak barrel where it fermented and aged in drunken bliss?"

"These are relatively subdued descriptions, still within the possibility of understanding," her grandmother answered, "I have read some that defy the verbal imagination of Shakespeare. Sometimes I was sorry for not having pad and pencil ready to copy those intemperate and fanciful descriptions. The extravagant adjectives would make great table conversation. I don't remember them all, but one of my favorite was of a Cabarnet, which had an 'attractive but curious nose, mulberry–ripeness, and the slightly pungent smell and taste of thoroughbred–stables.'"

Laura laughed with so much delight that some of the guests from neighboring tables looked over their shoulders to see what was so very amusing.

"I'm dying to know which part of the stables did he taste?" she said, when she gained control of herself again. "And what is exactly the differ-ence between the taste of a common stable in comparison to one where thoroughbreds are kept? The more expensive the horse the more perfumed its shit? Perfumed with mulberries yet! Estee never thought of that one," and she started to laugh again and Katharina joined her with a touch of marvel about herself. Tears and loss forgotten for the moment, she enjoyed sitting in a restaurant with this vivacious young woman, and almost unac-countably was able to giggle like a teenager about such a silly topic as the description of wines.

"But to find those exalted adjectives you'd have to go to a fancier place than the Pavilion. The more expensive the restaurant the more outrageous the wine description," she finally said.

"Yes, I know. And the more expensive the horse…" and without completing the sentence, Laura burst out laughing again, then added unexpectedly,—

"I am glad you came along to shop. I needed to do something different, because I was strangely depressed this morning."

"Anything unusual happen?" The motherly worries in Katharina stirred suddenly.

"Not really. But I had a strange dream, and the horror of it would not disappear," Laura said. "It was very confusing and I don't really remember the details, only the essence of it. I was climbing up to a ruined castle on top of a mountain. I was very scared, because the path was narrow and at certain stretches I could barely make it. The steps to the castle were broken; there were big gaps in the stonework, and it took great effort to climb higher. When I was almost at the top, a gate blocked my path. I could not open it, but noticed that the lower part was damaged, and where the planks fell out of the gate there was an opening. I crouched down to have a look and decided that I could squeeze through, but just barely. I was so helpless and so inadequate and for some reason, terribly scared. Perhaps I was fleeing from something. When I finally worked my way through, I found myself at the rim of a wild precipice. I was hanging on with all my strength, and someone was laughing harshly, and said, 'We don't ever win, we just survive.' I don't know whether he said it in so many words; you know how dreams are, half seen, half imagined, but I heard what he said, although I could not really understand it. I woke up with my heart beating madly; I was thirsty and frightened. And the impression, the fear of the dream would not dissipate, but hung on to me. I just had to get out and do something to take my mind off of it. What was the meaning of it? What did we survive? Was my dream a portent of some great danger?"

"Bad dreams are not necessarily harbingers of bad news. You learned in your introductory psychology classes all there is to know about the brain's activity during rest, and there is nothing sinister about it. Most dreams simply reflect in a distorted way our daytime thoughts, impressions and worries."

"I am not, cannot be, worried about precipices. For one thing, I never saw one. But what else is there that worried me so?"

"I don't know. Perhaps the task of buying the right gifts. Or the result of your midterms. Many things."

"Is that all?"

"You know that it is. But on the other hand, intellectually or historically speaking your dream is quite correct. Indeed, we all are survivors."

"Of what, grandmother?"

"Of uncounted years of struggles. If you consider that your parents, and their parents, and their parents and then theirs, all the way back for thousands and thousands of years survived in order for you to be born, then this surviving issue is truly a miracle. Think of all the famines, diseases, wars, subjugations, hunger, migrations, enslavement, childbirths, and displacement in all those centuries through which our ancestors survived and produced children. Amazingly, they did survive, otherwise we would not be here. No matter what their fate was, they gave birth, and made us their survivors. Looking at it in this way, our life is an unfathomable phenomenon, a miracle. Think of what stories these ancestors could tell us, what they have experienced, and what they have seen!"

"I'd love to know what an ancestor, let us say six generations ago, would have to say. Or another one three thousand years ago. Such a family saga would be the greatest book ever written. But what was the purpose for this stubborn survival? All this effort and suffering could not be for nothing!"

"You are right." Katharina looked at her granddaughter and experienced a stab of pain. This beautiful, well organized, goal oriented miracle of a child was disturbed, frightened and unsure about the purpose of existence. What bits of wisdom or guidelines could she give over a glass of wine, waiting for lunch? Whatever response she would make to the problem, which appeared clothed in a disturbing dream, would only trivialize the issue. Laura deserved a better answer, but Katharina was not prepared to give out pearls of wisdom at that time and in that place. Fortunately the waiter appeared with the bowls of lobster bisque, and this abruptly terminated the conversation. Laura turned her attention to the food, and the question of a minute ago seemed to have lost its significance.

But during the drive home Laura returned once more to their conversation at lunch. "Grandmother, did you find the answer to the question? I mean do you understand why our ancestors survived to finally produce you and me?"

"I think so. Sort of." Katharina answered slowly. "My life had content. I did worthwhile things, and tried to make the world a little better and a little less painful. I knew happiness, also the joy of giving and receiving. And I produced a wonderful daughter, who in turn produced two wonderful daughters and all of you are adding to the quality of this world."

"And you think this is enough?"

"Laura, I don't know. But I don't know a better reason for living, or a better answer to the existential question, so this will have to do. I never agonized about unanswerable questions; I just did what had to be done, and I did that to the best of my ability. I know it was not perfect, and by divine measures not even adequate, but given the circumstances and limitations, this is all I could do."

"You are a very wise woman."

"Not wise, just old. And as the years passed, I realized that I could neither save nor change the world, but I could and did make people feel better through my work. It is probably not nearly enough for salvation, but it would be a grave mistake to lose faith, or to stop creating, caring, loving because our human inadequacy There is much we don't understand and we often fall short of our own expectations. However, realizing that we are merely mortal is not a good reason to cease giving content and meaning to our everyday, often humdrum life."

Katharina stopped abruptly, as she realized that once again she said the right words but totally lacked conviction. She mouthed words without believing them any more, and felt hypocritical. Her neat, made–to–order, all–occasion speech was cheap and not worthy of Laura, or herself. The truth was that she saw no content and no meaning in her life, and felt guilty about sermonizing platitudes. It was never in her character to say things she did not believe. She stopped talking and silently asked her granddaughter's forgiveness for this crude and insincere preaching.

They were almost home, when Laura said hesitatingly, "Grandma, I had still an other reason to ask you to come with me today. I want to tell you something."

"I'm listening."

"I worry about Mom. She does not complain, but I noticed that when wine is served at the dinner table, she does not touch it. And I find anti–acid tablets and painkillers at her bedside table, in the kitchen, in the bath. She is so very thin and so exhausted that often she falls asleep on the couch while listening to the news. I know something is wrong."

"Did you talk to her about this?"

"Of course. She laughed and said that I am trying to play doctor, before I am qualified, and when I'll have two children, a husband and a job, none of them easy, I too will learn about heartburn and exhaustion."

"She is probably correct, but I'll talk to her about it."

"She was not terribly interested in my concern about her. But I know that something is very wrong with her. Remember, Mom is not home until the day after tomorrow. There is a conference for the big–wigs in Scottsdale. Don't ask me why Scottsdale, but that was the department's choice this quarter. They must like heat. Mom said she must go there and check up on things. That is why I took her to the airport – she likes to be there ages before any event commences, to work out all probable disasters before they happen. Or perhaps just to get away from us."

"Good, I will call her as soon as she is back." They arrived at the house and before Katharina stepped from the car, she reached over to kiss her granddaughter's face. "Laura, here is the key to your dream: you do have a grave worry. You worry about your mother."

"You think so? I do have to think about it, but you are probably right. I'd prefer the dream as a way of dealing with a fear, and not as the fore-shadowing of disaster." She looked at her grandmother with tenderness and added quietly, "You are so special and so beautiful!"

"Silly girl," Katharina laughed easily."I'm old, and my looks capitulated to the laws of gravity some time ago. I'm no longer beautiful."

"But you are!"

"Used to be, but it was a very long time ago. Before the Moon was born. Time is gone, and it left its marks all over me."

"You won't convince me, but thanks for the lunch and have a nice afternoon." And Laura was off.

The nagging feeling Katharina experienced after Alexa's e–mail, returned. Laura was right, her mother never complained, but that meant nothing. There are two kinds of frustrating patients: those who complain all the time, and those who never do. One of the blessings in pediatric medicine was that kids complained very clearly and often on top of their voices when they were sick, but never did when they were well. It made her job easier; she was not ensnared by too much, or too little information, while trying to make a diagnosis. Alexa always carried her pains silently.

Sunset

SIX

Katharina just started to prepare a simple dinner, when the doorbell rang. Rosie was getting ready to leave, but uneasy about an unannounced caller, she asked her to stay a few minutes, and also to heat the water for tea. Ever since Martin's death she felt insecure, or even afraid, when someone rang the doorbell unexpectedly. While he was alive she never suffered from such uneasy feelings, but now she was glad that the woman was still there.

When she opened the front door for a moment she was taken aback at seeing this big stranger at her threshold, and only after an awkward pause did she recognize the man as one of the recent employees from Martin's law firm. She could never understand why the partners hired Bill Jones in the first place, because he was as out of place in the office as a hippopotamus in a ballet school.

"We'll try him out," Martin shrugged. "I agree, it would be difficult to present him in polite company, but he does his work well. And shameful as it may sound, every law firm needs a ferret–type, and he sure is one."

So there stood bulky Mr. Bill Jones in her doorway, rather awkwardly oozing misplaced charm and the smell of stale tobacco, mingling with a cologne, which was created to suggest masculine strength and charm. At a low cost.

"Good evening, Mr. Jones. What a surprise! What brings you here?" she exclaimed and remained standing in the doorway uncertain and puzzled.

"May I come in?"

She did not answer, but moved away from the door letting him pass into the living room. He had bushy, reddish hair with matching eyebrows, neither attractive, and very small watery blue eyes. Gestapo officials must have looked like him before they started their interrogations, punctuated with strong physical statements, which often left their victims crippled, if not dead. His darting gaze was furtively inventorying the exquisite furnishings and art objects.

"Nice, really nice," he conceded. "It speaks of money. Lots of it."

"We liked to think that it speaks of taste and memories," she responded curtly.

"I don't see the difference. You need money for both."

Without invitation, he sat down and stared for a moment at the flames in the fireplace, then said again with obvious satisfaction, "Very nice." Katharina had the feeling he came to appraise, or to buy the house. His presence irritated her and she found it difficult to keep her voice and remarks more or less polite.

"I have not seen you since the funeral. How are things with you nowadays?" Katharina finally asked. Despite her deep aversion she tried to maintain the shallow conversation reserved for chance acquaintances, but it cost her considerable effort.

"Good. Even excellent. I am no longer with the firm, you know. I enjoy being free and am now in a position to realize my potentials."

"That is interesting," she mumbled, but added silently to herself, 'They finally kicked you out, Mr. Jones, and are now probably unemployed'; however, her expression remained closed, and she continued to gaze at him languidly with polite disinterest.

"You were surprised when I came, and did not try to hide it," he stated. "It is customary to say to a guest: 'Nice to see you, I'm glad you came by!' instead of showing guilty surprise."

"I'm sorry if I hurt your feelings, but I *was* surprised; however, I don't understand why I should feel guilty about it. In addition I don't think you were ever a friend of ours. I believe this is your first visit to our house."

"But I could be now. Your friend, I mean," he assured her. "And my remark about guilt is absolutely correct. According to office gossip, you are such an accomplished lady that when you just ignored the rules of good manners and showed insulting surprise, you acted against your principles and your breeding, hence the guilt. It was not polite, you know. Do you have anything to drink?" The request irritated her, and instead of getting up to serve him, as she would have done with any other guest, she merely pointed to the cart, where several bottles and glasses were lined up. He heaved his bulky self out of the easy chair and walked across the room with the flat–footed swinging gait of long–time waiters.

"Have you ever been in the army?" she asked abruptly.

"No. I was not qualified. Why do you ask?"

"No reason, just curious." Curious to know, if it was his flat feet, which disqualified him.

He studied the noble vignettes on the bottles, and finally decided to pour Scotch. She would not offer ice, or water, and he did not ask for it. Swirling the amber liquid in his glass, he stood for a while, then gulped half of the contents. After a moment of hesitation he lifted the bottle again and topped his tumbler. Slowly he walked back to the easy chair, and sat down with the comfortable movement of one, who plans to stay a long time.

"Do you mind if I smoke?" he asked.

"Yes I do. Our friends respect our disapproval of cigarettes. If they absolutely have to have one, they retire to the winter–garden to commit their sin. The plants can deal with the smoke better than we can." Unconsciously she used the plural, as if Martin were still alive. It gave her a measure of security against the uncomfortable intrusion. Mr. Jones looked at her in astonishment, but replaced the cigarette into the pack.

"You asked before what brought me here. Well, I thought you needed a friend now that you are alone and without a man, that's why I came," he told her leisurely.

"That is very kind of you Mr. Jones, but I do have friends, and I am not lonely."

"Still, Martin has been gone for half a year now, and it must be hard on you to be without a man." The alcohol started to work, and he was relaxed and daring. He leaned back, swirled the rest of his scotch and grinned at her in a revolting way. He probably wore the same expression on his face when he was about to carve the Christmas turkey. Tiny beads of perspiration appeared on his fat face while he looked at her with half–closed eyes. "You don't know me yet, but the women who do, think highly of me. Even Martin's private secretary was madly in love with me." He clucked his tongue as if he just remembered a very tasty dish. She was familiar with that nonsensical narcissism some members of either sex have in believing that everybody is in love with them. She was often wondering what gave them the courage for this conviction, and wanted to know if this was merely a sign of vanity, or perhaps a sort of mental imbalance, usually treated by professionals. But more than the concern about his monumental self–satisfaction, she was revolted and hurt by his remark. Is this what women living alone have to put up with, or was she just asking for it, when she let this man into her home?

She suddenly recalled the head nurse she met many, many years ago at the pediatric department of St. Vincent Hospital. Her husband was a WWII veteran and came home from the European theater with a decoration and paraplegia. While she would not have chosen either, she was a marvelous young woman, and took her vows seriously about "for better or worse", and "in sickness in and health", and did what had to be done. But once she had an outburst in a tone that was as close to tears as it was to laughter. "Men," she said with a shudder, which again could be equally due to revulsion or to suppressed mirth. "Doctors, male nurses, convalescing patients, and friends keep offering their services now that poor Tony cannot do his thing. I feel like puking." She was very pretty, had a feminine, rounded figure and a sweet disposition; Katharina imagined that she would have received propositions even if her husband would not have been paraplegic, and did not really take her complaint too seriously. Now after almost half a century, she was reconsidering the problem of the little nurse of long ago, and had a deep understanding for it. Yet, such a proposition sounded unbelievable and absolutely ridiculous at her age; although, she had a suspicion that this sort of crude harassment could be, regardless of age, the lot of women, who live without a man. She found it revolting.

At any rate, she was glad that Rosie was somewhere in the big house. The presence of Mr. Bill Jones was not comfortable. She was a fool to let him in. "How do you feel? Are you dating? Are you missing a man in your life?" He insisted, and never noticed the increasingly more frigid attitude of his hostess.

Blood rushed to her face and she stood up abruptly. A ferret, a weasel, just like Martin said, she thought angrily. His approach was uncouth and totally unacceptable.

She was almost seventy; an attractive, well preserved woman, but nonetheless, close to seventy. Mr. Jones was at least twenty years younger, probably married, unemployed and ill mannered. The situation was not just insulting, but also painfully ridiculous and potentially dangerous. What was he after? Her money? Her influence? Her connections? An excitement of a different kind? Blackmail? Did he consider her the booty to compensate for his loss at the firm? Did he think of her as a weak, easy prey? She felt nauseous.

"You would oblige me if you stopped taking my emotional pulse," she said coolly. "Your questions are impertinent, invasive and none of your business. It is getting late and I have plans. Good night, Mr. Jones."

He too stood and his face darkened, showing anger and disbelief. "Are you throwing me out, or are you bracing yourself to read to me chapter and verse?"

"Neither. I'm just ending this visit, which was long enough between two strangers." She was a doctor and used to the odor of sick babies, and it never bothered her. But the combination of stale tobacco smoke and alcohol, intensely mixed with that powerful and offensive cologne, which this fat, perspiring man emanated, made her reel.

"I don't belong to the hoity-toity society, but I heard that those who do belong are usually polite. You are not, and I'm speechless."

"What a blessing for the civilized world!"

"Have it your way," he shrugged, "But if you change your mind, I'm in the phonebook. Call me, and I'll come, even though your contempt is hard to forget or to forgive. Promise me to call."

"I can't see any reason for ever doing it." She shivered lightly and wished to physically push him out of her home.

"Lord, what have I done to you to earn this loathing?" he cried out. "I came with good intentions and you received me with the tenderness of a saguaro. I didn't ask for ice before, because your gaze was not just sufficient to cool the scotch, but hell could freeze by a single glance from you."

"Good night, Mr. Jones."

"I'm puzzled by your attitude. I could never really decide whether sarcasm is the weapon of choice for offensive, or defensive tactics. Are you scared, or just feeling combatant?"

"Good night, Mr. Jones." She stood in front of him, willowy, angry and determined, not unlike a cobra, which is ready to strike and only hesitates because its victim is so revoltingly unappetizing.

He then turned angrily and waddled down the front steps and along the walk in the front yard to his car. She still stood at the door, shivering. Never before did she have a similar experience, never before was she made to feel like an object that could be used, and the nastiness of it made her feel even more lonely and defenseless. She was so absorbed in her thoughts that the man walking up to her door took her by surprise.

"Ed Collins, your timing is perfect! Come in," she cried with exuberant relief.

"Hey, I know that we are old friends, but I was not prepared for this enthusiastic welcome," he said as he hugged her. "I just wanted to bring you a book, which I thought was really excellent. Who was that character leaving your house just now?"

"Come in, come in, and I'll tell all about him." She took his arm and closed the door behind him. "Come sit with me, my friend, and I'll bring us a pot of tea, which has the power to remedy all the inconsequential ills in this world."

"Was he...?"

"A pain in the nether regions? You bet. The kind that would have to be surgically removed. Nature's sad accident, the kind that Darwin failed to account for. A low–ranking guy in Martin's firm. Really, just a has–been, since apparently he was fired some time ago. He knocked on my door uninvited and unexpected, driven by less than honorable intentions. I felt uncomfortable and asked him to leave."

"Good girl. God was pleased to create a wide variety of animals on this planet, not all of them necessarily desirable. But this very variety of our world makes life so interesting here."

"I did not find my encounter with him interesting. He is scum, definitely lowlife, and if he has any sense of propriety, he must have hidden it somewhere in his alimentary canal. He had a sinister plan in the murkiest part of his mental shallows. Of course I would never have obliged him; therefore, for the rest of my life I'll be afraid of his retaliation. He was going to make the most of what he imagined to be my loneliness and vulnerable position after Martin's death, and made no effort to hide his intentions and his crude proposition. I'm glad you showed up in the very moment of my needing a sane, good man. You brought fresh air and security back into my home."

"You exaggerate."

But she was not. The friendship of Martin and Ed predated Katharina's marriage. The two men were at one time roommates at Harvard, and even though their professions took them into different paths, the friendship remained solid. They were a good foursome with Ed's lovely wife, Ruth, and together built memories to last a lifetime.

But then unexpectedly Ruth was dealt a life accident so enormous that the three of them were numbed by the enormity of it. Sporty, vivacious, always careful of her family's and her own health, she was struck down without the slightest regard for her excellent health record. Her family and friends were baffled. How could she, of all the people, so young, healthy and energetic be singled out to have a major brain hemorrhage? Katharina and Martin were the most important supports for Ed, sharing his fears and his hopes. Since then, and it has been five painful years, Ruth was existing in a barely conscious state, almost totally helpless, half of her body paralyzed, and in need of constant care. Ed would not hear of putting her into a home of any sort, regardless of its name or price tag, and arranged to have twenty–four hour nursing care right at home. He went into partnership with three other physicians in order to be able to be at her side at any given moment.

"We had an unforgettable quarter of a century together. She gave birth to, and raised two exceptional children. She gave all she had, and lived for us, for our children and for me," he explained when family and friends tried to convince him that Ruth belonged into a home, which could offer state of the art medical services. "There is no way in hell I would ever take from her that, which meant and still means everything to her. She always loved her home and she still does, and knows that I am near her. This comforts her. If you can talk at all about happiness in this tragic situation, I claim that she is, in her own special way, happy to be where she is. Therefore, she will stay at home, as long as I live."

He was as good as his word. He cut down on the workload in order to be able to spend more time with her, and for the same reason terminated almost all his social contacts, except for Martin and Katharina.

"You have no idea, what a lovely bride she was," he once told them. He loved to talk about Ruth as she was "before". "Radiant is the word. She did not arrive at the church in the sense ordinary people do. She appeared out of a cloud, or out of a dream. All of a sudden she was simply there at the door, as if she descended from heaven like a benediction, all wrapped in yards and yards of white lace, white flowers, and loveliness. I'll never forget the way she looked at that moment. She was a wonder, a gift, a treasure. And she was willing to share her magical self with me. We smiled at each other and said the words lightly: 'in sickness and in health' and knew not what they meant. 'Until death do us part,' we repeated happily, because death was no concern of ours, and it only happened to others. To old people, who already had their share of life. And then the unthinkable happened." He turned away then, to hide the tears.

When Martin died, Ed was at Katharina's side and they held hands at the funeral and cried, each for the unique, private sorrow life dealt them.

"Obviously he is a moron, and a very crude one at that," Ed now said his verdict about Mr. Jones."My guess is though that he won't bother you again, so try to forget him. I also think that he reached the end of a hopeless road, is desperate in his own subhuman way, and you seemed like a solution to his problems."

"But I am not!" she protested.

"Of course, you are not. The only reliable truth in life is that we are each responsible for the solution of our own problem. It is futile to expect outside help."

"You are so wrong about this, my friend. Have you forgotten how you helped me to endure Martin's death and all the agony after it? Were you not some sort of a solution for me?"

"No. Just a friend in need. But even the best of friends cannot ever be the solution. I still insist that only you alone can solve your problems." He looked at her with gentle, understanding and his gray eyes darkened from all the unexpressed emotions, fears, needs and sufferings. When he spoke again his voice was so full of tenderness that she wished to sink down next to him and cradle him in her arms."We had some beastly times, didn't we Kathy? And when will it ever end?"

Katharina hesitated for a moment, and then picked up the glass Jones left on the table and headed for the kitchen. There was reason and propriety to consider, and also the wish to keep the friendship pristine.

"Let me take the stinking glass of Mr. Jones to the kitchen, and release Rosie. I'll bring in the tea. If you still like to ruin yours with rum, please fetch the bottle from the cart."

After she poured the tea and put a few more logs into the fireplace, they sat for a while enjoying the quiet of the evening.

"You are a good person, Kathy," he said unexpectedly. "And you are exceptionally good to me and for me."

"We are friends," she responded. "Friends are like this."

"We had so many good times and lately so many bad times together," he said. "I don't know how I could have survived the tragedy of Ruth without the two of you." She did not respond. She could have told him again that she too leaned on him when Martin was ill and even more so after he died, but did not want to escalate the acts of friendship into a contest to see who gave more to the other.

"At times I'm at the end of my emotional reserves," he confessed after a thoughtful silence. "My training tells me that this happens to caregivers, but just knowing about the unavoidable negative thoughts is not enough to deal with them. Ruth's right to stay home, and to give her the best care are givens, not open for discussion. But Kathy, there are times, I feel that it is a terrible burden, and I wish to be without it. It isn't Ruthie I don't want; it is this terrible sadness, which is so hard to endure. She is here, but she is not. It was easier in the beginning, while we all hoped that somehow she would recover, and life could go on as before. I even tried to bargain with the Almighty. I was ready to settle for partial paralysis, but asked for full brain functions. It is now obvious that she never will recover, and will always remain at her present state of partial existence. I am a widower psychologically, but not physically."

"I understand the difficulties of giving care, even though I only had to live with that problem for three months with Martin, in contrast with the years you have spent with poor Ruthie."

"Kathy, you are the rock in my life. Our children, at the opposite coast, are totally overwhelmed with their children and with trying to make a living for themselves. They call of course, but ultimately I'm rowing alone in this boat going nowhere. I keep turning to you when in need of a safe grip, or when I need to talk non–professionally to another human being. Kathy, when I am sitting at Ruth's bedside and talk trivia to her, which she might or might not fully understand, I feel guilty, because I need a response, a dialog, which she can't give. And I know I would much rather spend the time with you. Do you understand?"

She poured more tea and then ignoring his statement, or the implication of it, asked after a while in a deceptively light tone, "Did you get an invitation to the medical congress in San Diego?"

"Why, yes. Why do you ask?"

"Because I think you should go."

"You know I can't. I can't leave Ruth alone."

"You have been saying this for years. But the time has come for you to do just that. Go. I'll move into your house to make you feel free to go. The nurses and I can give her the royal treatment."

"I can't accept it."

"Of course, you can. As a matter of fact you cannot afford not to accept it. You have worn yourself threadbare, and you need to get out. The congress is rich with unusual presentations. Add a few days to your stay to sleep or to play. Pamper yourself. Anyhow, I have nothing to do at this time."

"It is such a generous offer…"

"Fiddlesticks. It makes no difference to me where I sit watching the days go by, and you need to get out for a while. You won't do a favor for Ruthie if you crack up."

"The offer is tempting. But I wonder if I need all that information the congress is offering. Next month I'll be sixty–nine and am considering to give up practicing altogether. It is time."

"What do you plan to do? Sit down and wait for death? You are not cut out for that."

"You are right, of course, and I didn't plan to get petrified just yet. City Hospital is desperately trying to find doctors to teach, and that would appeal to me. I could still be in the profession, but teaching and guiding interns or residents in a hospital, as opposed to have a practice, would give me more time to spend with Ruth."

They sat quietly, watching the flames dance in the fireplace. A few well–placed lamps chased the darkness out, and Katharina's house became a cozy refuge. One could talk, or be silent, drink tea, feel the softness of down–filled pillows on the couch, see her book on the reading table and know what a home, where the spirit is still alive, feels like. Of course, worries did not go away, not even in her magical house, but they seemed less frightening, less overwhelming.

"Do you believe in a lasting friendship between a man and a woman?" he asked after a while. The question was not only unexpected, but out of context for this particular and unusual evening.

"At our age? Yes, most definitely. At Alexa's age? Perhaps. At my granddaughter's age? Definitely not."

"Why the division according to age?"

"Hormones get into it in a big way," she laughed, "And also the urge to explore new territories, which is usually enriched or complicated with a blind belief that each new affair is a novelty of cosmic magnitude. But that is history. At our age, we crave warmth and harmony. We want to share with a kindred spirit the emotional and intellectual treasures we stockpiled before senility or death would wipe it all out. The rest has lost most of its charm."

She drank her tea, and for a moment her thoughts wandered. The secret of her good marriage and her exceptional relationship with Alexandra were really based on friendship. And friendship with Ed was one of the few precious things she still cherished.

"So you think that at our age we have become sexless; therefore, friendship is quite possible?"

"Definitely. Think about us as we are sitting right now in an empty house, drinking tea in a companionable way, and then think where this would have taken us, say fifty years ago."

"Get your point. We wouldn't be talking for too long," he laughed and she loved to see him relax. He stirred the sugar in his tea with serious concentration.

"I don't know how general this is, but my physical self mirrors my spiritual self quite accurately," she remarked later. "I'm past passions, but love remained. I avoid the hateful scorching heat of the summer, but I'm content to sit on a garden bench and absorb the mild October sun."

"You are way ahead of me in that, Kathy. I'm close to seventy, but still do not enjoy the privilege of leisure, and autumn usually means an increased number of patients, who come for their flu shots."

"That is a real shame, and it worries me. We all have our limitations, but our days are numbered. Ed, you are no exception to the general rule. How long do you wish to wait to enjoy the warmth of the waning sun, and the spectacle of falling leaves?"

"That luxury is strictly controlled by time and by circumstances. On the other hand I do have your friendship, and so I am not missing the most important thing life offers. For this I am eternally grateful."

"Should I say, you are welcome? Lord, that would be trite, wouldn't it?"

"Not trite, just funny."

" Sometimes I reflect on our changing need for human closeness;

however, I have never come to a satisfactory conclusion. We use the word 'friendship' a great deal, often in a grossly sentimental way, but what do we really know about it? Friendship, like letter writing, has become such an old–fashioned thing. So few practice it in the true sense, and we know too little about both."

"You are forgetting the Christmas letters!" His eyes sparkled and she knew he was teasing her.

"Composing immodest laundry lists of enviable trips, fabulous achievements, and superhuman children does not qualify as an art, nor are these really 'letters' to friends in the traditional sense. Madame Sévigné is probably turning in her grave non–stop from November to mid–January. These letters are sent in the hope of turning the recipient green with envy, and have nothing to do with the nobler side of our selves," she retorted. "I'm convinced that the fine arts of friendship and of letter writing, like the maintaining of salons in Paris, belong to the more civilized world of the past."

Skillfully she guided the conversation out of dangerous waters, yet knew exactly what he meant. She too wondered sometimes about her relationship to Ed. They were very close, always have been, but with Martin totally and Ruth partially removed from the playfield, their closeness could spell danger. And of course there was that age thing. What is the meaning of septuagenarian emotions and how valid are these? Yet, loneliness cries ever louder for remedies. Susan fell in love, of course, but she is different and it proves nothing. And of course, despite their absence, there are, and always will be Martin and Ruth. She valued Ed's friendship and was scared to muddle it. Life would be so impoverished without him, but carelessness could instantly shatter the companionship. She could not afford one more loss.

"Forgive me, old girl," Ed said reaching for her hand. "I didn't mean to disturb your peace of mind. And I would not like to be asked to leave, like Mr. Jones was, when he stepped on forbidden ground. But loneliness does strange things to a man, who is undoubtedly a social animal, and only feels well balanced, when it has the closeness of its kind."

"Which is why solitary confinement in a prison is the harshest punishment. Ed, my home is open to you at all times, and I hope yours is equally open to me. The open door is imperative, because I'm moving in to lady–sit Ruthie. Actually, I think she needs me less than you do. Without my taking over her care, out of sheer guilt you would never fly to San Diego. And no matter what, you must get away for a few days. I'm saying this as a friend and also as a physician."

"You are not mad at me?"

"Darling Ed, if I would be, you'd hear it loud and clear."

"Katharina, I won't ever again mention the terrors of my isolation, nor the graces of my foolish hopes. But I would like to clear an issue, before it could be misunderstood. Please understand that I am not using you as a child uses his security blanket. You are a marvelous woman and when I feel myself drawn to you, I am not looking for a surrogate wife or mother, nor do I seek a human tranquilizer. I simply bask in the warmth you are offering. I would never demean you by relegating you into the role of a stand–in. I value your friendship. And I am scared to lose it. Do you understand what I am trying to convey in the most awkward manner possible?"

"Of course I do. As long as you promise to get on the phone first thing in the morning and make the arrangements for San Diego."

SEVEN

And so Katharina moved to Ed's house, and sat for hours at Ruth's bed, holding her hand, talking. With each passing hour she learned more about Ed's dark pain. Ruth, wasted but alive, rested mostly motionlessly on her high–quality satin sheets, her face more like a mask. The eyes, the windows to the soul, seemed brooding; the light of recognition and intelligence almost, but not completely gone. She conveyed immense sadness, as if she had looked into a dark cavern and could not forget what she saw there.

"It is so easy to take care of poor Mrs. Collins. Too easy," the day nurse said. She and Katharina helped Ruth from her bed and attempted to move her across the room in an effort to exercise her half–paralyzed body. She leaned her light frame against the two women helping her, and obediently did as she was told. But the lame leg was unwilling to participate, and she dragged it across the floor like a piece of useless appendage, which it was. She patiently suffered the enforced, awkward walk, just as she suffered the exercises of the physical therapist. "She cooperates the best she can; yet I wish she would give me a heap of trouble. That at least would show sign of interest, or a flicker of true life. I'd welcome an angry outburst, tears, abuse, anything, but this patient and soulless cooperation."

"Ruthie, I'm sure Ed told you that you'll have to put up with me for a few days," Katharina told her after she was helped back into her bed. "You do know, don't you, that Ed went to a medical congress. I'll be staying with you for a few days. See, I got centuries older and sadder since you last saw me, but I hope you still remember me. I'm Katharina." There was a flicker in Ruthie's eyes and it encouraged Katharina to go on. "We used to have so much fun together, you, Ed, Martin and I. Remember when one summer we went to Martha's Vineyard and in the evening wanted to build a fire at the beach, but none of us had a lighter or a book of matches...?"

And Katharina talked for a long time in a soft, clear voice. She talked about their common experiences, about her grandchildren, about Alexa and Martin, and when she could not think of anything else to say, she recited poetry to her. Her fifth grade teacher was a devoted disciplinarian, and Katharina always had a free spirit; therefore, often in trouble. As a consequence, she had to memorize enough poems to last a lifetime.

Nearing seventy, she had a hard time remembering the numbers of her two phones, of her social security card, or of the license plate on her car, but she remembered most of the poems. Ruth did not respond, but she kept gazing at Katharina with the same intent look with which some babies scrutinize the world around them, but decline to comment on it.

"Ruthie, the way you are looking at me, I know that you understand me, and that you want to tell me something. Why else would you look at me for such extraordinarily long stretches? Can you tell me that you hear me? Can you squeeze my hand?" Ruthie looked on silently.

"Ruthie, Ed tells me that you can and do respond at times. Do give me a sign. Like this," and she squeezed the wasted little hand. Ruth, like a little wax statue, was motionless for a short while, but then Katharina felt a small push against her fingers. With tears in her eyes she bent down and kissed her friend's face. "Thank you Ruthie. Now I know that you heard me. Rest well and find peace in your sleep. Ruthie, you must know that we love you. Martin is gone, but Ed and I love you and care for you. I'll be next door to you, and the nurse stays in your room all night. You are safe with us here." There again was a light squeeze on Katharina's hand, a silent response.

"Good girl, Ruthie. You'll make it yet."

When she returned to her room for the night, she paced up and down for a while, then sat down at the desk and wrote into her diary.

"I know, God yes, I now know, what this must be for Ed. After Martin died, I mourned and still mourn for him, but there was a closure. The horrible, gnawing pain will cease one day, as it must, and then I can start living again, although I know that it would never be quite the same. But Ed? Where does it leave him? She is dead and not dead. He mourns, but never totally. He nurses his sad sorrow along with a stubborn hope and a reluctant acceptance. Recoveries, or at least partial ones, have been reported. She had all the therapy and still is getting them. There must be brain pathways left, which are not damaged, and one day they might start working and transmitting impulses. I fear that they won't, and I believe that despite the brave hope he still holds, he has no illusions either. But then again, who knows for sure? It happened before. That strange look of hers is still alive in a special way, as if she looked out at the world from a different dimension. There was also that squeeze of the hand. She still communicates. But how much? Did she understand what I told her, or is she like a pet, which learns a few commands, knows how to respond to them, but that is its absolute limitation? If she would be totally unconscious, if she could not do a thing, she then would be dead to the world. But it is not so. She is only catastrophically impaired, but alive and responding at some level. How long can she keep this

up? And how long can he live with this? Ed, dear Ed, he bravely lives a life beyond self, beyond personal consideration, just because he is dead serious about his vow to love her in sickness and in health. He takes his responsibility like a man. This is one of the attributes of saints and heroes. And he does it gladly and out of conviction, and does not feel that living the way he does is self–mortification. Well, at least he does not feel that way most of the time.

And I thought that Martin's death was the worst thing that could have happened. Please God, and please Martin, forgive me for thinking it, but this is much worse. Much worse."

She closed her diary, and for the first time since his death she went to bed crying for somebody else's sorrow.

Sunset

EIGHT

The invitation to the exhibit of Lettie's collection of paintings was graceful. The fine ivory paper and its torn edge was nicely set off by a pair of narrow bands of gold and deep blue. Katharina read the simple text with pleasure, because it was so much like Lettie to stand back and have her work speak for itself. Elegant simplicity and modesty without a trace of disfiguring self–aggrandizement were her trademarks, and these made her personality shine high above lesser souls. This would be a memorable and well–deserved day of celebration.

Sarah and Katharina arrived before the gallery opened for the public, and Lettie offered a private viewing of her collection, consisting mostly of still life and landscape paintings. There were only a few portraits, but one caught their eyes immediately, because it was not just striking in its beauty, but also because it was painted in a markedly different style from the rest. The white–haired gentle man in a bishop's garb looked at them with ageless patience from the frame. His fine hands with tapered fingers were reposing over an unadorned prayer book; around his lips and in the eyes lurked peaceful merriment and tender encouragement.

"Lettie, you surprise me! Who is he? Some distinguished relative, of whom you never spoke? He doesn't look like someone you should be ashamed of!" remarked Katharina.

"No relation. It is just my idea of how Saint Sulpice would have looked," she answered simply. "He is my favorite saint, you know. The patron saint of late–bloomers. The painting is my small way of thanking him. I used my father's best friend for a model. This is the only painting not for sale," she added.

"The things you care about, amaze me," said Sarah, and gave a quick squeeze to Lettie's hand. Her gaze returned for a moment to the portrait. The painting had a strange power to captivate the observer. The figure was surrounded by darkness, but an evocative light illuminated the face and the expressive hands. With the calculated artistic skill of mixing light and darkness on the canvas, the old man appeared mystical, in the possession of some secret, and was lifted above the commonplace world. The figure was mysterious with a solemn aura; the expression of the face carried spirituality and kindness. "Too bad, that you want to keep him for yourself," Sarah said lightly, without her usual biting sarcasm. "Every failing mortal should have a copy of it in his bedroom, because your Sulpice radiates the kind of power, which could help anyone face any Monday morning, any time." She then turned from the painting and scrutinized Lettie's flawless floor length and obviously expensive black suit and white silk blouse. Lettie was truly beautiful, mostly because she was in possession of the only fool–proof, absolutely reliable and powerful beauty aid on the planet earth: happiness. She appeared years younger; her eyes sparkled, her movements became free and graceful, she radiated energy, her face expressed one great emotion of unclouded joy. "But I'm glad that beside your religious and artistic preoccupations you found something besides sweatshirts, baggy pants and drab turtlenecks in your closets to wear for tonight," concluded Sarah with obvious approval. "You really look the part now. I was afraid we'll have to be embarrassed on account of your haphazard attire."

"You forget that I used to dress for occasions," Lettie answered mildly. "On the other hand, it is a generally accepted notion that artists are individualistic, even eccentric, so I don't think people would have been shocked to see me in my habitual painting uniform."

The doors were opened and the gallery started to fill with people, who walked around with the usual reserved and serious attention, which successfully covered their caution about offering a premature opinion about an unknown artist. This was strange territory and one had to be careful not to commit a blunder, which would never be forgiven by the cognoscenti.

In the general subdued gathering Susan burst in, like an exotic flower of splendid beauty. She wore a raspberry pink suit with black trim, black gloves, black stockings, and a rather large black hat with pink ribbons and roses. She looked like a smashing model in one of the slick fashion magazines. Age, either young or old, could not be detected on her face, on her figure, or in her movements; she was glamorously, elegantly ageless. For a moment Lettie's paintings receded from the general point of focus as the visitors stared at this gorgeous woman. The man with her was equally noteworthy, but while Susan was exciting, he was dignified. They were obviously very happy together.

"No wonder Sue could hook a guy! She looks and acts like a damned supernova," Sarah sighed, but without envy.

"And she also has the virtue of virtues," Katharina responded, "A kind and loving heart, enlivened with a passion for life."

"And you my friend, cannot pass up an opportunity to say something kind about a person. I can't do it. Kindness and bad weather bring out my contrariness. But I love you for doing it."

Susan and her escort moved to the circle of friends, introductions were made, banalities expressed. Lettie's manager (after all, she *did* have one!) took her by the arm to introduce her to the visitors. As she stepped up to the microphone, a hushed silence fell over the gallery.

She was calm, poised, and proceeded to surprise her friends with a side of her personality, which was almost totally foreign to them.

While married to her husband she was habitually presented as the proverbial "little woman", the perfect wife of great charm, of very little worldly wisdom and not much intelligence, who tended the home fires with love and thoughtfulness, but was little else than a benign household goddess, not too different from Ibsen's Nora Helmer, whose job was to attend to the welfare of her husband, and to provide the proper environment for his greatness. Her place, after she emerged from the kitchen and served the cocktails, saw to the seating, and orchestrated the serving of the first course, was the benign and muted background. She was a useful, undemanding decoration of the house, and people very seldom took notice of her. He, being a member of the chosen sex, occupied himself with the truly important questions of the world and of his business. He was admired and respected, and nobody expected his perfect little wife, who quietly served elaborate meals to the guests, to add a single word to his unquestionable wisdom. After his death she was the quiet, retiring widow in her cottage home, and her softly spoken opinions were kindly accepted and then promptly ignored.

Now she greeted her guests graciously, then without either pretensions, or false humility spoke of her art to an attentive audience.

"Some women produce excellent food, so very necessary for life; or else bear beautiful children, just as necessary for the survival of the species," she said with charming simplicity. "Everyone does what she can under given circumstances. In the dynamic period between complete maturity and useless senility, I am no longer called upon to produce food or children, so I create art. By the way, art to me is as necessary as food…

"Notoriously bad painters have often turned into serious critics and pedantic experts, who attempt then to explain the art of others. They usually start by categorizing the artist into easily recognizable cubbyholes. They believe it can be done and do it enthusiastically, and from there proceed to dissect, analyze and explain every single brush stroke. Impressionism, to which school most of my work might be attributed, was thus academized into lethal boredom. I think I am correct in believing that this fanatic trend to dissect every piece of art probably was the kiss of death to the wonderful, exciting movement in all the arts in the early twentieth century. Too many words and theories took away from it the very things it was supposed to represent, which were (and still are) emotions and impressions, carefully stripped of sentimentality, banality, of half truths and of untruths. For me at least, art is spiritual, and sensual, as opposed to intellectual, scientific or dogmatic.

"I agree of course that informed, professional evaluation of works of art is imperative, and the personal reaction of the viewer is part of the artistic experience. But, and I wish to emphasize this, forced interpretation is the most negative critique there is. In effect it says: 'This art work is woefully incomplete; it failed in its quest to show something; therefore, I, the critic, must tell you what it is all about.' If this would be the actual case, if the artwork could not speak for itself, the artist might as well give up her art and turn to basket weaving. This is how I see it.

"For this reason, I will not talk about my paintings. I sincerely hope that they'll speak for themselves and won't need any interpretations.

"In general, I might mention the goals of an artist, which are not any different from the goals of the average person trying to give meaning to life. The list includes a search for unexalted reality and truth, an attempt to stay away from clichés, and an endeavor to penetrate below the surface of things. Most of us, weather we are housewives, accountants, artists, bank clerks, authors, office managers, or gardeners seek the human, the personal element, and turn from the lethally uncritical collective state of mind. In the context of artistic expression, we are mostly against the trend, which seems dedicated to destroy beauty, reason, and love, and which on top of it also tries to use art in place of a therapist.

"In addition some of us, who are dedicated to painting and are more intent on creating than on preaching, take what we can from the example and the genius of the great pathfinders, such as Cézanne, and go about our work without falling into the trap of becoming picture–makers, trend–setters, or message–conveyors. We only think about the object and its emotional impact on us, and wish to enter into a silent dialogue with those viewers, who observe and understand their environment. Cézanne's paintings of the mountain of Sainte–Victoire and the countryside near his home in the town of Aix are beacons to guide us, and inspire us for finding new and intricate solutions.

"We, who chose this path, are of course not great artists by world standards, but we are artists nonetheless, and we try to capture the significance of form and its sublime emotional content.

"I hope that my paintings are complete without having to explain philosophical or intellectual contents, which would not only be far more difficult then painting them, but which content they posses only as much as all our endeavors in life possess them. Please walk around and see what I have seen, and feel what I have felt. May I hope that some of these paintings will recall your own memories, and will sharpen your perception of the beautiful world around you. Thank you."

Enthusiastic applause followed, and a throng of interested art lovers surrounded her.

"I'll be damned," Sarah said. "Did you follow her high–flying, artsy discourse? Lettie in her impossible baggy pants and shapeless shirts knows Cézanne so intimately that one becomes jealous of her secret life."

Refreshments were served and the selection of finger foods occupied Sarah for a few minutes, and only after she picked a few choice bits did she continue to talk. "How come her husband tried all his life to diminish her into the little doll–like housewife? Lettie was always smarter than he ever was, God rest his soul. I don't mean that pompous little Dunstan moved his lips while reading, if you know what I mean, but still she is smarter, if for no other reason than just for outliving him and so finally coming into her own. Psychologists call this self–actualization, if I am not mistaken. And now she can create paintings, for which people are willing to dish out outrageous sums, and she talks about them like a college professor. Where does that put him?"

"More power to our talented, smart cookie," Katharina responded with genuine warmth in her voice. "Her husband was either blind, or else suffered from a gigantic dose of inferiority complex. The only cure he could find for it was to cut her down to a size he could work with. Nevertheless, he was much admired and was considered to be a deep thinker."

"Bah, you don't believe this bunk yourself, and are only saying it, because you must have a kind word about everybody, including the devil and its dark relatives. Kathy, you are so sharp, you could not have missed that he was nothing more than an arid pedant, a stuffed shirt. People flocked gladly to him, because of his charming home and well–set table, neither of which was his doing."

Katharina did not wish to dwell on the subject, and was saved when she spotted Alexa and her two daughters sweeping into the gallery somewhat late.

"To get this family together is an exercise in futility. One cannot decide what to wear, and the other is not able to tear herself away from the university," she whispered to her mother. "And of course I can never find my car keys."

"Glad you could make it in the end, but it is too bad you missed Lettie's introduction, it was really nice."

"You'll tell me all about it later."

They walked around looking at the paintings and were sincerely impressed. In the past they saw Lettie at work once in a while, and have seen examples of her luminous landscapes, but to see them so, displayed together, with perfectly placed lights, was an overwhelming experience.

"No doubt about it, the woman is deep and mysterious, always has been," Sarah finally said. "The point is that we never realized just how deep and how mysterious."

"I find that mysterious women have so much charm," Karen agreed. "The problem is that you need the necessary characteristics for it. I'd love to ooze feminine mystique, but then I kiss and tell."

"And then tell again," Laura put in, but not unkindly.

They were again in the little office of the gallery, waiting for the last visitors to depart. Laura went out to the car and returned with a basket. To everyone's amusement she removed from it fluted glasses, crackers, sour cream, tiny spoons, a crystal bowl with ice, Beluga, and bottles of champagne.

"Child, did you rob a bank?" Susan inquired.

"My contribution to your triumphant show," Laura explained to Lettie, who just entered with her manager, a portly gentleman, who was introduced as Harry Lasky. "One has to celebrate a victory, which does not happen every day, and when finally it does come along, it must be properly appreciated."

"You are right, Pumpkin," Susan said, and she seemed to encase Karen with a maternally loving glance. "But perhaps life would be much richer if we would also celebrate failures and disasters. Certainly there are many more of them, and if we would include the bad days as occasions for high celebrations we could immensely increase the number of our joyful festivities. We could also perhaps discover that failures and losses are not necessarily devastating."

Katharina blushed, because she felt that Susan was alluding to her grief. Mr. Lasky, ignoring the awkward silence, opened a bottle and filled the glasses.

"This has been a true victory, and here go my congratulations and best wishes. I knew that Nicolette was good, but even I did not count with the response of the visitors. We sold and sold, and will be selling. Many happy returns," he said solemnly.

"Your introduction was very impressive," congratulated Katharina too. "It was wonderful and I don't just congratulate, but also thank you for it." Lettie smiled and briefly hugged Katharina, but as always, she shrank from receiving compliments, and was more comfortable when she could hand them to others. It was time to change the subject.

"Laura dear," she said turning to the young woman, "This is such a wonderful and thoughtful gesture on your part, thank you so much for the goodies," Lettie said graciously. Laura's gesture touched her.

"Don't mention it; the pleasure was all mine. Also, I owe it to you as an act of contrition."

"What are you talking about, child?"

"To atone for my sin of feeling jealous of you."

"Of me? My dear, that is quite impossible!"

"Not really. I envy the gift of being able to creatively express yourself. Also I think that creating something is another way of taking care of your soul. I so very much wish I had some talent. If I could do something perfectly…"

"But Laura, first of all, perfection is such a huge word and so very relative. Need I tell you that it is mostly just an illusion? Nobody is perfect, my child. And you are doing creative things! You play the piano, you write, I bet that you even paint."

"Of course," Laura said, and although she accompanied her statement with an easy laugh, there was a hint of sadness in her voice. "I can do a lot of things, but am master of none. This is frustrating and disappointing. When I am sad I play Bach for an hour or two, but am glad to be alone in the house, so that others can't hear it. Playing his toccatas, fugues and fantasias help me over my unhappiness, but the sound of it would be intense pain for one, who knows music. My paintings are pathetic little watercolors with nothing to say, and my writing is confined to boring term papers, which are usually read not even by the professor, but by one his graduate students. I so wish I could do one single thing really well, like you do. So have some caviar! It is for the celebration of your talent and success; it is also my version of a love feast, an agapé." She was serious and acutely embarrassed by it.

"Going to school and earning great grades does not count?" Lettie asked.

"Not really. Most people can learn stuff if they put their minds to it, but only the gifted ones can create, like you do. I admire you and hope that you create more of the same. Or create something different, if you are so inclined. But don't ever stop. You have such divine talent."

"Amen," said Mr. Lasky.

From the background Katharina looked at this granddaughter for a long, time. She had no idea that this brilliant and gifted child was suffering from pangs of inadequacy and restless yearnings. While Karen's life wobbled, Laura earned top grades, had a definite goal. She was usually the calm center in a storm. She took care of herself and watched the mechanics of her family with keen eyes and with empathy, but never gave any indication that not all was well in Paradise, that she too had unfulfilled dreams and yearnings.

But Laura already turned to Susan and engaged her in a lively conversation. Katharina was wondering whether the fleeting discontent on the young face she observed was true, or merely a ghost her imagination made up, because she loved her so much.

NINE

The weather turned unpleasantly wet and cold. Katharina moved restlessly from room to room, but the warmth and light of former days were gone. In an effort to dispel the nagging emptiness, she built fires in the study, the living room and the dining room. While occupied with the task, the demons receded somewhat, but when she finally sank into her reading chair, the pain emerged once again. The ringing of the phone brought relief. Anything would be better than the familiar feeling of sinking into depression.

"This damned weather is chewing up the last few nerves I have left", the caller shouted.

"Sarah?"

"Whom did you expect? Laura Bush?"

"Glad to hear from you. The fog and rain made me edgy too, and your call came like a blessing."

"Don't praise the day until the sun has set. It is only ten in the morning, too early to talk about blessings. The sky has still plenty of time to crash down upon unsuspecting heads. I would like to have you over for lunch today."

"Am I to assume that you found your kitchen, Sarah?""

"Just because I am a vegetarian does not mean that I don't like to eat, or don't know how to cook. As a matter of fact, I am pretty good in both departments, an overachiever even, as you probably observed already. It is also confirmed by my constant complaints about my ballooning body. Be here by noon. It will be just the two of us." She hung up before Katharina had a chance to either thank, or find an excuse for not going.

The invitation was surprising and unprecedented. Sarah was always very busy, running from one meeting to the next, and did not socialize much. Katharina found the unexpected lunch date slightly odd, but was glad for it. Despite her rough edges and the disinclination for socially acceptable communication, Sarah had a heart of gold and an uncompromising honesty, which Katharina valued.

"Glad you showed your face," Sarah greeted her guest. "Sorry I hung up so promptly, but I was not about to accept a lame excuse for not coming to see me today. I thought if I hang up you wouldn't have the nerve to call me back and decline."

"You know I wouldn't have," lied Katharina. "I welcomed your call and thank you for the invitation."

"Cut the chicken shit."

"How are you, Sarah?"

"I have seen better days, and even then I wasn't jumping for joy."

She ushered Katharina into the breakfast room and immediately served tall glasses of tomato juice.

"Bloody Mary," she explained. "Lavishly enriched. Your body is a temple, a sacred vessel, and watch what you put into it, and so on. You heard the phony litany before. The hell with it. I'm no longer a believer. Cheers!" Her guest barely touched the drink, but Sarah was again filling up her own glass. Katharina looked at her with concern.

She did not know about a drinking problem.

"No, Old Girl, don't look at me like a damned doctor. I am not an alcoholic, and you know it," Sarah said when she noticed the concern in her guest's eyes. She busied herself with serving the lunch, and added quietly, "It is just that I need a few drinks nowadays."

The creamy soup was a delightful combination of carrots, apples, ginger, wine, coconut milk and curry; the spinach and cottage cheese quiche was wonderful, the crust melted in the mouth, the filling was light and spiced just right. The assortment of salad greens was dressed with a delicate mixture of raspberry vinegar and hazelnut oil. She served with it a light pale Riesling of excellent quality. It was a fabulous lunch and Katharina praised it lavishly, but the conversation was light and of no consequence. Sarah was troubled and unusually subdued.

Finally they finished lunch and the kitchen was filled with the aroma of freshly ground and perked coffee. Sarah was a fanatic when it came to the black brew. The coffee beans, the water, the imported Italian pot, in which she pressure cooked it, all had to be select and perfect, according to her own high and somewhat quixotic standards. She cleared the table, and then served the espresso in delicate gold–rimmed demitasses, accompanied by a miniature mountain of whipped cream.

"What hides under the pristine landscape of snow, disguised as cream?"

"Charlotte Russe."

"And what happened to your theory of the body being a sanctuary, and eating the right things a way of life?"

"I told you already. The hell with it," Sarah said as she placed a bottle of Grand Marnier and one of Kahlúa on the table.

"Easy, Sarah! I have to drive home yet, and need to be able to read the street signs."

"Please yourself. I don't have to drive anywhere and will imbibe as much as needed to anesthetize me."

"You don't need much more to achieve that. Will you finally tell me why this sudden invitation?"

"Yes I will. I invited you, because I want to make a confession, but not before lunch. This simple meal took enough of my time and energy, so I did not want it wasted. I hoped that you'd enjoy it before heavy topics are dished out."

"That bad?" Katharina smiled, since she was sure that the topic would involve Susan's impending marriage.

"For me, bad enough." She paused and regarded the coffee in her cup for a little while before she spoke again. "I have cancer."

The words were spoken and they filled the silent room like evil spirits. Pandora's wretched box of miseries was opened. A response was needed, but how to say it? The kitchen was as before, and the coffee was still perfuming the air with its fragrance, yet everything appeared in a different light. Sarah looked tired and frightened and her friend, the doctor, who had years of experience in announcing catastrophic diagnoses, sat there mortified, groping for words.

"Alas, you lost your legendary bedside manners! Who would have thought this possible?" Sarah said, and it was almost a jeer, but one that was dangerously close to tears. "Our cool, professional Katharina lost her cool when her friend's boobs are in danger! While you gather your wits, let me tell you the gory details."

And she did, from beginning to end. Only then was Katharina able to respond.

"Sarah, it was detected in time, and breast cancer is the most curable of all of them."

"I know. This is what the doctor said, but of course, we were not discussing his boobs, nor those of his wife or daughters. From where I stand, it looks different. Bad. Bad and utterly frightening. But I did not just ask you so I can cry on your shoulders, although I am not too far from it. I am asking you, no I'm begging you, to be with me during the ordeal. I don't want Marisa's useless sophistication. I want a friend who is as solid as a rock, has as much savoir–faire as you have, and is as good as an angel. Kathy, I can't go through this alone. Will you be there when I hurt and when I puke? And will you be there to tell me the truth, and nothing but the truth?"

"Of course I will. And I feel honored that you trust me and asked me. When are you scheduled to enter the hospital?"

"Tomorrow."

"I'll be there, but you better stop your home–made anesthesia right now."

"Surgery is not until the day after."

"I figured, but you'll mess up the preliminary tests with all that alcohol."

"Don't leave me yet. Kathy, I'm scared. I am afraid of the future, of the pain, of complications, of metastases, and other things, which I cannot even pronounce, let alone understand. I can't sleep, think straight, or do anything worthwhile. I am not mentally deranged; I just feel like it. Stay with me, please."

"I'll stay if you want me, or else you can come home with me. I'll take you to the hospital tomorrow."

Sarah was like a child, who is afraid in the dark. Surprisingly she eagerly accepted the invitation.

After Sarah's admittance, Katharina became almost a fixture in the hospital. Lettie too came daily, and even though Susan would depart before Sarah was out of the hospital, she too sat in the waiting room with her two friends while Sarah was in surgery.

Katharina stayed with her friend almost constantly during the first difficult few days after surgery, and visited her daily during the remarkably good recovery period. In a very short time Sarah in the voice and style of a field marshal, was already teasing the doctors and the nurses, and by the end of the week she made imperious phone calls to her several committee members, and in general had everybody dancing for her. Even the prospect of possible follow–up therapy did not dampen her spirit.

"I only hope I never will have to repay you in the same coin," Sarah said in an unusually emotional moment while holding on to Katharina's hand. "I pray that God may grant you a healthy life without the indignity of having to periodically chop off parts of you. See, we don't die at once. That would be too merciful, and certainly reeking of a mediocre, sentimental drama. No, we go bit by bit, everybody according to his own schedule and genetic inclinations. First go the teeth, then the eyes, the hearing, the skin, the joints, muscle tone, sex, boobs, uterus, ovaries, hair, memory, mind. After a certain age we are facing a series of degrading losses, both physical and psychological. They go one by one, sometimes in tandem. Self–assurance, hope, an unshakable trust in the future, the belief that all people are good, and everything will turn out for the best are all eroding. What is left? By the time we exit this world we are about as bereft, helpless and weak as when we entered it. Except nobody thinks that we are as cute as we were in those first months and years of our life. When we fill our diapers and chuck up our dinner, nobody is gurgling loving incantations over us while changing our gown and washing our ass. It is a hell of a way to exit."

"Yes, but didn't we have fun in the meantime?"

"I can hardly remember it any more. A good thing though that this happened to me, and not to Susan. It would have dampened her amorous fling quite badly. Well at least I will not have to worry any more about my aging, hanging breasts." But she had tears in her eyes. "Think of it, to be concerned with this at my age," she added apologetically.

"Why shouldn't you? Go ahead and grieve for it a little, but not too much. When a part of us is taken, we mourn it one way or another. It is difficult to let go. Do you know that when I finally agreed to have Alexa's long braids cut, I couldn't pitch them? I'm saving them to this day. It was part of her, part of her childhood. When she was young I washed and combed it so many times, braided it in so many ways, put ribbons into it. She hated her hair. Hated to have tangles and cried while I brushed it for her. It took forever to air dry it, and she would not let me use the blower. Keeping it nice and shiny was an ordeal for both of us. Yet, when they were cut off, I could not let them go. The braids are in a box, wrapped in tissue paper and I will never throw them away. So tell me, Sarah, how would you judge my mental state? By the way, that box would be another thing, which would not fit into a Lautner–style architectural perfection I mentioned a few days ago." Sarah was actually smiling at this.

"I hope you are not suggesting that I save my boobs in a box, wrapped up in tissue paper?"

"Formaldehyde would be more appropriate, but I would advise against it. "

"The thought of a scarred, boobless chest revolts me. Can you understand it?"

"Of course I can, I just told you that it is all right to feel this way. On the other hand, fortunately we don't live in a topless society, so who'll notice what is missing? And I'll be there when we get the prosthesis and buy that special bra for you to make you look younger and spiffier than my grand-daughters. Then we'll go out and celebrate this brand new passage."

"Do you suppose the stuffing would keep me afloat? You know, I never learned how to swim."

"It's worth a try."

"You are kind, generous, and a true friend, and I am sorry that I'm whining now. But Katharina, I don't really know what I want."

"What do you mean?"

"The way I see it, I only have two options. Either I could wish to live into venerable old age, maybe about one hundred years, and on the way to that milestone lose my faculties one by one, until everything is gone and I am nothing more than a real burden to Marisa. Not a pretty picture. Or I could die soon, and be done with it. But death scares me worse than losing my boobs. The problem is, I can't think of a third option." Sarah stopped talking. It was very unlike her to reveal so much of her emotions. To admit fear or confusion was a weakness, and she would rather bluster and cuss than admit helplessness. In an attempt to lighten the conversation she later added a closure in her usual flip style. "It seems to me that in the end, due to advanced medical technology, most likely we'll get it all: extended life, *and* sickness, *and* senility, *and* death. And you won't even be consulted about the options. I don't approve of the final scene, written so carelessly. A better and more elegant ending would be imperative, but that damned Reaper is not only getting impatient at my bedside, it also lacks style in a big way. He is nothing but a cheap hacker, good only for mass–market paperbacks."

"Now you are really unfair to that lonely gentleman and his job, which he might not like any more than you do."

"Oh Kathy, don't tell me you'd have a good word even for him?" But her eyes were closing and she had no strength left for a good argument.

"Lucky for you Sarah, because this problem does not have to be solved by you. The truth is that there is no choice left for us between life and death, unless we consider suicide, which of course, we are not. Other than that, the final decision is more or less taken from us."

But Sarah drifted off and probably did not hear a word of it. Katharina looked at her friend's listless, yellowish hands resting on the cover, and at the dark shadows on her face. The closed eyes seemed to have sunk into the tired, old face. A sudden deep sadness swept over her, although she was fairly sure that Sarah would pull through this time. This time. But how long would she feel relieved for having escaped?

Man was not granted eternal life on this Earth, and the Reaper is ever ready for the harvest, because it was so ordained. The entire process follows a script with relatively few variations for the animal and the plant kingdom, and so the drama is endlessly repeated. To call death by the rather poetic name of "Reaper", is overused, but the metaphor is very appropriate.

The germinated seed miraculously survives; good rains nourish it and merciless winds strengthen it. Days turn into nights, and the nights into days again, and the newly grown wheat–stalk lifts its head to heaven in youthfully proud challenge. The sun and the clouds go about their household tasks in an organized, dependable way. Ignoring the existence of the plant, and lacking all personal emotions and attachments to it, but like well trained nannies, they do see conscientiously to its daily needs. And as the plant matures and it finally realizes its own insignificance, it hangs its heavy head in sincere humility. And now it is ripe for the harvest, ready for the Reaper. End of the drama. Looking at it this way, the similarity between the life schedule of plant and man is obvious, nor does it appear that an individual plant, or a mortal for that matter, is all that important in the universal scheme of things.

But Katharina suddenly had enough of the doomsday picture, which had overtaken her in the semidarkness of the sickroom. With a newly awakening pro–life optimism she stubbornly argued against her own gloomy thoughts, and closed her reflections with a hopeful note. One stalk of wheat is truly insignificant, she thought, but millions of sheaves are able to nourish the world.

Sarah was fast asleep, and after a while Katharina tiptoed from her room.

Sunset

TEN

A week later an arctic blast moved over the region and gusty winds tore at the branches. Winter finally arrived and it did it with the energy of a beginner. Snow mixed with rain coated the roads and driving was gradually advancing from hazardous to dangerous.

There was an accident ahead on the highway and Gary was stuck in the rush hour traffic jam. He tried to call home, but the line was busy. Karen was probably talking to one of her friends. This could take forever. Alexa's cell phone was turned off, and her phone at work was ringing ten, twelve times, but nobody picked it up. Laura was probably still at the library of the university, with her cell phone off, and also could not be reached. "Damn," he fumed aloud in the idling car, "I'm paying a king's ransom for all those phones, but when I need to get in touch with any of them, I might as well forget it. I could connect to the red phone in the White House easier than reaching my over-phoned home." Frustrated and marginally worried he inched his way ahead, then exited at the next intersection and made it home through the back roads.

The house was dark. He picked up the mail at the end of the driveway and drove the car into the triple garage, and registered with surprise that Alexa's car was there. She must have arrived home in the meantime. Dropping the mail on the table in the hall he called, "Honey, I'm home." There was no answer. Turning on the lights as he went, he almost missed her. Actually, it was the dangling wall phone in the kitchen that first caught his attention.

She was lying unconscious in a pool of blood on the white tiles of the kitchen in a contorted position, her head resting on a low plastic stool. It was always underfoot in the kitchen, but she would not part with it, because she used it to reach the higher shelves. Gary complained about it periodically, because it seemed too unstable and hence dangerous, but she always argued that the kitchen was built for giants, not for average size women, and the upper shelves were not made for decoration, but for practical use. She had to reach them somehow. The stepping stool stayed in the kitchen, and now her head rested on it and it was splattered with blood. Lots of it.

For a second the fear and horror numbed him before he could pick up the dangling phone to dial 911. "My wife… she is bleeding… unconscious…she either fell or was murdered… send an ambulance," he screamed. The operator had a hard time getting the address right. Only then did he bend down to look into her pale, lifeless face.

There was an awful lot of blood on the floor, even on the wall under the phone, but it did not come from the head or the chest as he expected. It was coming from her mouth. There was a foul odor around her and he noticed a blood soaked bath towel on the floor under her head. Then he heard the sirens.

Two policemen, a detective type, and the team from the ambulance arrived together and were ringing the doorbell; Gary was immediately flooded with questions. The ambulance team wanted to know things about Alexa's state of health, which Gary could not really answer, and the police and the detective acted as if he would be the prime suspect in the murder of his wife, which he probably was. He knew the questions from countless movies about crimes, and recognized from the same source the dour, closed faces, and the arrogant, insulting voices of the interrogators. Where were you in the afternoon? An hour ago? Do you have witnesses in regard to your whereabouts? Did you have an argument with your wife? Was anybody home at the time of the crime? And so on. Gary knew from the movies that they were considering circumstantial evidence. For want of a better suspect, accuse the person who found the body. If the finder is the spouse, so much the better. Spouses usually have more reasons to kill than casual acquaintances or strangers.

Gary told them that he was in the office, and then was stuck in a traffic jam, and no, he had no witnesses to that effect. He had a bitter argument with her the day before, but wisely did not offer this incriminating information. The row they had was of a personal nature and certainly had nothing to do with anyone wanting to kill her. Speaking about it would only muddle the issue. He tried to bend down to his unconscious wife, but an officer pulled him back. He was sorry to intrude on his frightened emotional state, he said with routine coldness, but there were some more pertinent questions about the case.

Gary turned to him in a white hot rage, "For God's sake, can't you leave me alone? This is not a 'case'! This is my wife! I don't even know if she is alive!" he screamed. The detective looked at him with malevolent eyes. The suspect is nervous. Rather suspicious. Only the most routine criminals remain calm when confronted; the rest gets nervous. Real nervous. He continued to make notes on his pad.

Meanwhile the ambulance team surrounded the motionless body of Alexa and did magic things with the tools of their trade, calling out professional mumble–jumble to each other. The stretcher was placed next to her and while the assistants lifted her light body on it, the young doctor turned to the defenders of law and order, who were still busily taking notes and photos about the case, and kept questioning the evident suspect.

"Relax pals. There is no crime here. The lady is in severe shock from internal hemorrhages. That is bleeding in our language, you know. Probably ulcers. We'll take her now to the University Hospital's ICU. She'll definitely need blood transfusion, tests, probably surgery. If you have further question, contact the hospital."

Gary stood immobilized in the midst of the commotion.

"Smart lady, your wife," one of the ambulance attendants told him with sympathy before following his team. "She probably knew that she was about to pass out as she slid to the floor, and put her head on that stool. Lucky for her. With such profuse, torrential bleeding, aspiration of blood could have been an ugly scene. It was a very close call."

She was whisked out of the house, and the ambulance tore away with flashing lights and the siren wailing. The policemen completed the report about the false alarm. Gary called his mother–in–law.

"Katharina, I don't know how to tell you this without giving you a coronary. When I came home I found Alexandra unconscious in a pool of blood. She was just taken to the hospital. The University hospital that is. "

"Oh, my God!"

"Exactly how I feel. The emergency doctor thought that perhaps ulcers caused the bleeding, but of course, he could not be sure before some tests are made. I had no idea she had ulcers. Why are women so damned brave? They complain when the garbage isn't taken out, but quietly bleed to death without a word of warning to anyone. Apparently she tried to phone for help when she passed out."

"Was she alone?"

"Yes. The girls aren't home. I was stuck in a traffic jam. I heard on the radio just as I arrived home that it has not yet been resolved. God knows what would have happened if I did not exit at Wilson Road and worked my way home through the side streets. Oh God, I hope I was not too late!"

Gary couldn't stop talking. The events of the evening were so frightening that he still could not understand them, and in an effort to explain things fled into compulsive talking.

"I don't know where the girls are," he continued. "I want to be in the hospital with Alexa, but I need to stay here and break the news to them personally, whenever they get home. I don't want them racing alone and frightened to the hospital. And Katharina, the doctor indicated that she'll need blood. Lots of it. I did have hepatitis and can't donate blood."

" I can, and am also a gallon donor with a special card and privileges for my immediate family. Was she conscious when you found her?"

"No. At least I don't think so. I am not coping very well, Katharina."

"Stay where you are. I'll drive directly to the hospital. I think it is very wise to wait for the girls. It is dinnertime, so they should show up presently. See you later at the hospital."

"I'm frightened."

"Hang in there."

The receptionist at the emergency admittance greeted her cordially.

"Dr. Caldwell, how good to see you! You haven't been here much since you retired…" she bubbled the customary prefabricated polite phrases, but then stopped as she remembered that indeed Katharina was in the hospital daily, although not as a practicing physician, but as a wife visiting her dying husband, and then just recently again, holding her sick friend's hand for days on end. The receptionist was flustered.

"It is all right, Gloria. I am slowly getting over the worst of it, also, my friend is going to be well again."

"I am so very sorry. How are you coping?"

"Not too well just now. My daughter was brought in per ambulance…" She stopped herself then. She wiped the frightened expression from her face, and slipped into the safe professional role. She hated when well-meaning people perceived her as an emotional basket case.

"Alexandra McKenney?" asked Gloria.

"Right."

"Oh…" the receptionist stammered. "They took her up to the ICU."

"I know. Here is my gallon card and I want to start giving more blood right away, because I can't do much else at this time. She'll need it, and I would only be in their way up there now. But I'd like to be informed of her condition as it develops."

"I'll see to that," Gloria promised.

Katharina was ushered into a room, given a tall glass of orange juice and helped to a cot. Time crawled, or perhaps even stood still. She finished her juice and tried to pray, but her thoughts swirled incoherently and her gaze kept returning to the large white clock on the wall. The hand on the blank face moved just as sluggishly as before. Later a nurse entered with a tray, and inserted a needle to draw blood while beaming a professional and deferential smile. Mrs. McKenney was taken care by an excellent team made up of a gastroenterologist, a surgeon with expertise in GI problems, an anesthesiologist, several assisting doctors, a cardiologist and a group of highly skilled nurses, she assured Katharina. Somehow it was not terribly reassuring to know that her daughter needed all those professionals. One of the doctors would soon come and give a detailed report, the nurse added. Katharina should not worry meanwhile. Of course not. This young and pretty nurse probably could not comprehend what it feels like when one's child is found unconscious in a pool of blood on the kitchen floor, and nobody around to help her. What did she know about the black worry left behind after the ambulance speeds away? She probably could not imagine all the doomsday scenarios a physician is able to conjure up when facing sudden and profuse internal bleeding. Especially if the patient happens to be the only, beloved daughter.

She watched her blood, this simple red fluid, flow into the bottle. A true miracle, this blood. It nourishes, cherishes, and sustains life, corrects insults which daily invade the body, and fights off corruption. A miracle that might save Alexa's life. How medicine changes, she thought. A few generations ago blood was drawn from sick patients to let the bad humors leave the body. Now blood is given to bring back the failing life. Herrick's words came to mind:

> *Fair–pledges of fruitful tree,*
> *Why do ye fail so fast?*
> *Your date is not so past;*
> *But you may stay yet here a while,*
> *To blush and gently smile; and go at last.*

With her free hand she wiped away the tears. Alexa can't fail now. She never did before. Alexandra, the iron lady, outspoken but full of wit, assertive, but always ready to help. Successful in whatever she touched, a golden person, brimming over with love and understanding. Year after year, ever since she was a teenager, on her own birthday she gave a bouquet of flowers to her mother with a card. The gesture revealed her sensitivity and romantic side, which was so surprising from this down–to–earth, no nonsense woman running a formidable business venture, with a funny rejoinder for every bad turn or stupidity she experienced. Every year on that day she thanked her mother for having and for raising her, and explained that while she was the lucky one to be born, it was Katharina, who was the heroine, and who made all the difference; therefore, the celebration really belonged to the one, who gave life, and not to the one who received the gift of it.

After what seemed an agonizingly long time, one of the assistant doctors came in to remove the needle from her arm, and to give the promised report about Alexa's condition. The initial diagnosis of a bleeding ulcer was correct. They were able to stop the bleeding and to stabilize her, and were now debating whether surgery, or some other treatment would work best. So after all, Alexa the obedient, was not at all obedient and did not follow her mother's and daughter's plea to visit her physician, Katharina thought bitterly. Once again she was not aggressive enough.

She walked to the waiting room and the girls flew into her arms. "Grandma, will she be OK?" they sobbed.

"Of course she will. The worst is over. Fortunately, your father found her in the nick of time, and they can fix her now. She will need a long time to recuperate, but yes, she'll make it."

"So good to hear you say it," said Gary, who aged during the last hours. "One of her doctors was here a little while ago to talk to us. Frankly I was not sure whether he talked Latin or English or perhaps Arabic. Half the words he threw at me I did not know. What the hell are a Salem pump and a panendescopy? And what sort of a cuss word is an endotracheal intubation? He was explaining the options of surgery and of endoscopic coagulation as if I knew the difference."

"Poor culturally challenged darling," Katharina teased him tenderly, "You obviously never watched E.R., otherwise you would be well–informed about every medical term and some."

"I want her to get well, but don't ask me to understand the terms, or to choose between two things, neither of which would I want performed on me, or on her."

"Gary, don't let the big words frighten you. As medicine becomes more complex, new words have to be invented for various instruments and procedures. That is all. She has a rather vicious ulcer, but she is now stable. They are making sure that she does not bleed again. Later they will choose the method best suited to bring about a quick recovery and permanent healing. By now she is medicated enough so she doesn't really mind the instrumentations done to her, thank the Lord."

She stopped talking and wished to feel as calm as she showed herself to her family.

"Can we see her?" Karen wanted to know.

"Later, Darling, we have to wait a bit. They are working on her and we would be very much in the way. Besides, she is medicated just now, and probably asleep, which she needs badly."

Finally they were gowned and were permitted, two at a time, to enter the ICU. Karen was grasping her grandmother's arm so tightly that she actually caused pain. They stood quietly at Alexa's bed and watched the tubes and machines connected to her slight body; these were the anchors holding her to life. The room was murky dark, only the green numbers and lines on the monitors trembled with uncertain energy; steel and glass implements eerily reflected the impersonal and weak glow. Tears were rolling down Karen's cheeks as she bent down and kissed her mother's hand resting on the cover. "Mom, please get well", she whispered softly, but Alexa did not open her eyes.

"She obviously responds well to the medications," Katharina explained to her granddaughter. "Rest is the best thing for her now. The most capable doctors in town are taking care of her, and she is a fighter. With or without surgery she will be fine. This looks very dramatic, but considering everything else, we can be relieved, because an ulcer is one of those things that can be fixed. I was afraid of much worse."

The nurse whispered that their time is up.

"We just came," Karen objected.

"I know this was a very short visit. But a little later you can come back again, and maybe you'll be able to talk to her then."

As they left Karen looked back one more time into the room with its futuristic equipments and the motionless form of her mother.

"She looks so still," she whispered. "I am not used to see her any other way except in perpetual motion."

"Leave it up to the painkillers and relaxants to slow down even the fastest human whirlwind."

"I could never be a doctor," Karen said with a shudder. "I could never poke, cut, or cause pain. I know it has to be done and that it helps the patient, but I could not do it. It makes me sick just to look at all this."

"Not unusual. We all feel a certain amount of horror for some jobs. I for example would die if I had to earn my bread in a coalmine. I am so claustrophobic that I'd go mad the first five minutes down there. That also goes for an astronaut's suit. Or if I would be drafted to serve in the army! That is a regular nightmare. And I could never work with electricity." As she talked, she glanced sideways at Karen. Her color came back and by the time they reached the end of the corridor, she was her own self again. The irrelevant chatter distracted her mind for a moment, and she regained her balance.

"She will be all right, won't she?"

"Of course she will. Especially if she'll learn to take better care of herself. If need be, we'll force her to do that."

"Still, all those tubes and machines… and what if she needs surgery after all?"

"Then they'll do it, and do it well. However, nowadays they have so many alternatives to surgery that I doubt they'd take that route."

All four of them tried to be at the hospital as much as possible. Karen took the mornings, Laura came after school, and Gary in the evening. Katharina practically lived in the hospital and commuted between the rooms of Sarah and Alexa. Meanwhile Sarah's release from the hospital was fast approaching. Katharina offered her home for the recuperation period, but started to worry about how she would divide her time between the two patients.

The days that followed were difficult. Bleeding had started once again, and even after receiving unit after unit of blood transfusions Alexa's blood pressure and pulse rate were again unstable. Ed Collins, the friend in need, was once again at Katharina's side.

"Kathy, I know that you worry about your daughter. I just saw her again, was involved in the consultation, and wanted to talk to you about her," he told her over the phone.

"Thanks, friend."

"Kathy, she is a sick cookie and is not responding as well to the treatments as it was hoped. We are still not considering surgery, but this repeated bleeding has us worried. We would like to treat her as we did before, because she deserves a full life after it is over, with as few restrictions in the future as possible. However, if she does not respond soon, we'll have to go in. You know that delaying the procedure might worsen the prognosis. We are in a bind and are watching her constantly. I think—or perhaps 'hope' is a better word for it—that we can pull her through without surgery, but she is not out of the woods by far. I just wanted to let you know, because if surgery is the way we'll go, it will have to be done the minute she shows the need for it."

"Does Gary know?"

"Vaguely. I don't know how much he absorbed from what I told him. He is pretty broken up."

"I'll talk to him."

"Don't alarm him. Let's just keep our fingers crossed until morning. If she pulls through this night, we might win this battle without the mighty scalpel. For this we all hope."

"Thanks again Ed. You are a true friend."

"I regret that I could not tell you something more cheerful. But tomorrow is another day, and when I next call, I'll be bursting with good news. This is a promise."

After he hung up, Katharina sat for a long time and tried to line up the options, and imagine post–surgical syndromes. In pediatrics she had next to no experience with ulcers, and wished that she knew more about it, but a strange fatigue took possession of her and she did not move to search for more information. She bent her head over her folded hands and cried quietly. Beautiful, vibrant Alexa, barely fifty, could suffer any or all the ordeals of weight loss, (losing weight from where? She had nothing to spare), severe food restrictions, anemia, vomiting, maldigestion, dumping syndrome, and a host of other things, including the recurrence of the ulcer and more surgery. No and never, she thought. Alexa has to respond to the treatments, she must get by without surgery, no matter how invasive the treatments are right now. She is young. A long stretch of her life is still ahead of her.

She then called Gary and talked to him, as she always did since Alexa's illness: hope–inspiring, positive, professionally unworried and unhurried. When they hung up he felt better. She did not, and was watching the shadows in the room until the morning's light came.

She recalled what Bella, one of her friends, said about the worries of a mother. Bella lived across the street from her married daughter. The daughter was a TV news announcer and kept late hours.

"Winter nights are the worst," the friend explained. "I listen simultaneously to the radio and to the television and do not draw the curtains so I can watch her driveway. Rooted at the window and watching the snow come down, I imagine how it collects on the icy road, how visibility decreases, how cars slip and slide, and I wait with a prayer for the miracle of her headlights to show up. One by one the lights go out in her house. Her children and husband go to sleep peacefully, while I still stand at the window watching, waiting and praying for her. They sleep peacefully while I am sick with worry. So tell me, when are mothers freed from responsibility and worry? Do we keep on worrying until death do us part? When does the husband take over?"

"As you said, my dear. Our worries stop the minute we die," Katharina answered. She wondered whether Gary too was awake through the night praying and worrying.

But next morning Ed called again, and his report was a bit more cheerful, a bit more promising. Alexa was stable again, was awake and wanted to see her mother. Katharina was at her bedside in half an hour.

"Why couldn't I get an elegant disease, where I don't puke, have no pain, just languish away? Where they don't poke horrible things down my throat and don't destroy my veins?" Her voice was hoarse from the instrumentation and she was pale, limp, and the radiant glow from face and eyes was gone. She lifted her thin arm to show the intravenous tubes. "I must look like a voodoo doll with pins stuck in her..."

"To tell the truth, you looked better at Lettie's bridal party, but perhaps not quite as interesting as you look now. Take it easy, Love. I know it is easier said than done, but your doctors are determined to pull you through without surgery. It seems they are winning too."

"Much obliged. It is good that you are here," she said and dozed off immediately. Katharina did not move from her bedside the rest of the day and most of the night, but it was by then obvious that Alexa was improving. Only then, when danger was over, did a soothing softness, a blend of thanksgiving and relief give peace to Katharina. Until then she was emotionally numb and instead of true prayers, she only repeated a wordless plea, which sounded something like: "No, no, no."

As a matter of fact, considering the rough beginning, Alexandra's recovery was better than expected. The therapy was aggressively pursued, and the ulcer, which was much larger than previously suspected, started to heal nicely. As she left the hospital she was still wobbly and very pale, but definitely healing and out of danger.

Sarah too was released from the hospital, and after some polite and insincere resistance from Marisa, she moved in with Katharina during her final recovery. Katharina spent her days split between her home with convalescing Sarah, and taking care of her daughter.

"I spend more time in my car nowadays than I ever did," she told Ed.

"Need I tell you that in the meanwhile you should also take care of your own self? If not for your own sake, then at least please think of those, who rely upon your help, like your two patients. They'll need you for a long time yet."

"Yes, doctor. However, both patients are doing well and they are less trouble every day."

"Glad to hear that. But what if Sarah would end up needing chemo after all? Rumor has it that it's no picnic. You just might have your hands full again."

"Yes, sir."

"Another thing. Have you seen today's paper yet?"

"No. Do we have a new war somewhere?"

"Probably. But the short notice in the back of the paper might interest you more at this time. Mr. Bill Jones committed suicide." Katharina stared at Ed for a long moment, and the color left her cheeks. She started to shiver.

"How terrible!"

"The paper did not say much and did not even speculate about the reason for it."

"Ed, then you were right about him. He must have been at the end of his rope when he came to see me. And I turned him down with sarcasm and revulsion."

"Kathy, for heaven's sake, don't you now take his problem personally too, and don't start sliding down the treacherous tunnel of unfounded guilt. You were not elected to solve everybody's personal problems." He put his arms around her until she calmed down somewhat. "The man came to you, and he came under false pretenses. He did not come openly and did not say what he wanted. He wanted to manipulate you to serve his own dark purposes. Actually we don't even know for sure why he visited you. Or why he committed suicide. You felt uncomfortable and asked him to leave. You couldn't have done anything better under the circumstances, especially since you had no idea that I was about to ring your doorbell."

"But perhaps I shouldn't have been so very abrupt with him."

"Have you forgotten what you taught your daughter over and over again? You told her 'If you feel scared, or uncomfortable with a man, run. Flee. Scream. Get out. Throw him out. Instincts usually don't fool you.' I can still hear you say it to her. You asked him to leave for this very same reason. He scared you, or at least made you feel uncomfortable. Quit feeling guilty."

"It still makes me feel awful that I didn't recognize the cry for help."

"Because he wasn't crying at all. He was drinking and making himself into a grand nuisance. You couldn't have helped him, because you did not know him or his troubles. And he certainly didn't state his problems."

"Perhaps he would have, given more time. Perhaps he was about to say it."

"It was wrong timing anyhow, because before he could have told you his life story, I would have been already at your door. I don't think he would have shared it with me as easily as he would have with you. And quit deluding yourself, that you could straighten out every messed up life on the planet."

"Not every one of them, Ed, only those who turn to me for help. It is a shock, believe me." She hugged him for a farewell, and turned abruptly. "Take care of yourself, and squeeze Ruthie's hand for me."

Sunset

ELEVEN

Katharina and Sarah were good company for each other, and Sarah soon spent increasingly more time in the kitchen, almost converting her friend to vegetarianism.

It was good to have someone in the house. The two women formed the habit of drinking their afternoon tea in the winter–garden, where they enjoyed the warmth collected there from the fading sun.

"Was your marriage really as good as we thought it was?" Sarah asked at one time.

"Yes," Katharina answered simply. "We were very much alike, and had none of the perennial problems which can destroy the most hopeful marriages, such as money issues, in–laws, children, or professional problems. We met after we both survived a long period of loneliness, and we had the identical memories of good marriages behind us. Our interests were alike, so were our dislikes. Among other things I adored his tenderness and sense of wit; he loved my calm and flexibility. We also knew, during every moment of our shared life, how good we had it, and this made it even better, or keener. How about your marriage?"

"Not so perfect," she answered slowly. "I think we were weary of each other. Even little things appeared frustrating and irritating, but we lied bravely to each other and to the world. For some reason it seemed very important to keep up appearances, and much of our energy had gone into maintaining it."

Katharina knew that they were straying to dangerous ground. She was always very circumspect and discreet about her personal life, and respected the privacy of others. She was not sure that she wanted to hear a secret, which could turn out to be a double–edged sword. A confession made wholeheartedly today, might cause remorse a while later. Friendships have foundered before in the murky water of regretted confidences; however, Sarah apparently had a need to talk about it, and so despite her resolve, Katharina asked , "Were you unhappy?"

"Not acutely. Just unfulfilled and always on the watch for his outbursts. All my life I was very honest and straightforward, and suffered intensely about the lie of happiness we presented to the world. It was all fake. Such a farce. I hate that we lived our life on two levels. One was the reality of our marriage, and the other the sanitized version we showed the world. In truth, he was very manipulative and I was the traditional wife accommodating his need to be in the leading role. At least outwardly. My life was not enhanced by him; as a matter of fact, he regularly diminished me. But I was not really unhappy in the sense of having to take pills, crying through the nights, or totally depending on a shrink. And then, you see, we had our moments. We had them, and then it was good. We did have our dreams and visions, only we never did anything about them, just spoke of them in Walter Mitty fashion." She shrugged and then added,"It is only in bad novels or movies, when things are either all good, or all bad. Real life is a mixture of both."

She refilled their cups, sat down again and fussed for a while with the sugar, the cream, and the little cakes Katharina offered with the tea, before she picked up the story again. "Have you been to Italy? I mean, have you seen La Solfatara, above the town of Pozzuoli?" Katharina has not, and shook her head to indicate it. Sarah sighed, then continued. "I have, because Albert was a nature enthusiast, and would not have missed it for the world. Had you seen it, you would know what my marriage was like."

"I don't understand."

'Solfatara is a semi–extinct volcano," Sarah explained. "When you arrive at the top, you actually descend into a circular, flat area, which is completely surrounded by a fairly high embankment. I suppose it is really the filled–up crater of the old volcano. The ground is smooth, covered by a white powdery stuff. At first glance it is peaceful there, almost idyllic, but then you see that the ground is pockmarked with fissures. The devil's kitchen is steaming underneath, and his grandmother is probably cooking up their dinner from her evil ingredients. You notice this without fail, because mud is bubbling from the fissures, mixed with hot sulphureous gases and foul vapors. And it is hot there. The tour guide will tell you that some of the largest fumaroles reach 324 Fahrenheit. That is hot. You could roast a chicken on that. You keep hopping from one foot to the other in your thin–soled summer sandals and hope to get away with only second–degree burns. Then the guide would throw a stone, or stamp with his foot, and you hear a hollow, eerie sound, as if there was nothing but an endless depth of infernal heat under a thin layer of earth where you stand. You think that any moment the ground will crack under you, and you'll disappear into an unbelievable horror. You feel with every fiber of your body that it is not a safe place, and suddenly you really want to get the hell out of there. My marriage was La Solfatara."

"Did you ever talk to him about it?" A small, uneasy pause.

"Not directly. Believe it or not, there was a time in my life, when I was afraid of confrontations, afraid of speaking up, mortally afraid of his reaction. La Solfatara." She was silent for a while with a strange expression on her face, as if she looked at something unexpected and unpleasant. "No, I never talked directly about the problems, but I invented people and situations, and related my fabrications as if they were stories of others, nothing to do with him. Not a very original approach, I admit. Thomas More did the same thing in his *Utopia*, when he attributed the evil political deeds to Francis I., which were actually committed by Henry VIII., while fervently hoping that despite his monstrous egotism, Henry would see the connection. Speaking out, yet circumventing the problem in this way, perhaps he also hoped to save his own neck, at least for a while. I had the same stubborn and grossly naive hope."

"Did it work?"

"Are you kidding?" Sarah laughed with bitterness, tinged with derision. "It did not work with Henry, and it also did not work with my husband. In henriesque fashion, he too was outraged that people would behave in such a way, and never saw that in my stories he was the main actor, and the actions he condemned were his own. I guess some people, or perhaps most, while highly critical of others, never perceive their own faults, their own body odor, their own dullness, or vulgarity. He certainly was one of these."

"And?"

"End of story. More lost his head, and I sunk diligently into silent passivity. And now I compensate for my stupid meekness by being as busy as a gerbil on an activity wheel, and telling off people. I am not scared any more, and I guess I want to get even."

"I understand."

"I thought that so did I. And then you know what happened? He died, and suddenly I was devastated and even after all this time I am still at a loss without him. Can you understand this? I can't. I could not live with him, and now I miss him. I totally forgot about his need for the regularly occurring combats, our mutual dissatisfactions, his addiction to conflict, and the fact that while married I always felt better when he was not around. I forgot those ills as completely as I have forgotten the birth pains. I now wish that I could rewind the time and start over again, and be a more loving, a more accepting wife. I think now I understand what made him the way he was, and I also know that he could never have changed. I think that today I would not judge him so harshly."

"Are you awarding him this understanding as a posthumous gift?"

"Better that, than none at all."

"Sometimes we overdo this solicitous understanding, this overlooking of meanness in others. If we explain away and forgive all sins, we might not do such a great favor for anybody. I am all for excusing shortcomings, but sometimes I do wonder how far this should go. By permitting others to be mean, we give them the green light for more of the same. Flagellating ourselves for the sins of others is a form of spiritual hypochondria and as such, not very healthy. And finally, did death bestow a new dignity and saintliness upon him? Why judge him differently now?" Katharina was not sure that what she said was what she really believed, but Sarah was torn, and the last thing she needed was the burden of guilt. Also, she did not really know Sarah's husband, who was smart and usually entertaining, but always with an air of detachment, which hindered friendships to develop. She was not in a position to judge.

"Oh, Kathy, he was a man, that is why he was what he was. Men are just different from us, and it takes us a lifetime to learn this. I think lesbians have got it right. They discovered what the rest of us did not learn in seven decades, namely that women are easier to live with, are more loving, more supporting, less combatant, have neater household habits, and cook better. Also they clean up the kitchen after their cooking is done. At any rate, it is too late for all this regretting. But I wonder sometimes, whether Marisa turned out to be so cold and so self–centered, because she learned next to nothing from us."

The two women listened to the silence for a while. They were comfortable with each other. Despite the return of her bubbling energy Sarah too could sink into periods of meditation. They watched the sun move from plant to plant, and enjoyed the light as it occasionally glanced off a glass sun–catcher, which Katharina hung on the windows to discourage the birds from committing suicide on the glass plates.

"Anyhow, then came the deluge, the locusts, earthquakes small and large, and finally the unsatisfying end. But there is something else," Sarah said continuing the conversation as if there was no lengthy pause since her last statements.

"I'm listening."

"Katharina, my husband was an abused child. He never spoke of it. Never. I had no idea. His family seemed so normal, so well put together. No one suspected it. We tend to be believe that abuse happens in the slums, and not in mansions with Greek columns, and stone urns spilling evergreens at the entrance. But the elegant façade was no protection for the two boys, victims of a violent father and a severely unbalanced mother. The first time Al talked about his private hell was when he was dying. Imagine, carrying that burden through an entire life! He and his brother were brutally abused, and I don't mean harsh discipline. The abuse was both physical and emotional and extraordinarily cruel. His brother, three years older than my husband, committed suicide at age fourteen. This tragic event made my husband's young life even more unbearable and lonely, and he ran away twice. Both times he was brought back, and both times the authorities failed to look and see, and certainly failed to act. As he told me the story, gasping for breath between the chapters of horror, I realized how much this man suffered, and what he must have endured in order to survive. Had I known about his life tragedy, I would have felt differently toward him. But he could never talk about it. He was like a friend of ours, who had been to the Korean War. Al could never talk about his private hell either. They both dealt with their memories privately. My husband was blustery and combatant to be sure, but not in the chivalrous way of Roland at Roncesvalles, if you know what I mean. It wasn't bravery or masculine virility that made him so. It hailed from a damaged childhood and a damaged soul. He was covering up, or acting out past miseries. Whatever. Still, I think now I understand him."

"Sarah, understanding why something is wrong, does not make it easier to endure it. Do you really believe that knowing the cause for the toothache will make the pain disappear? Knowing why he acted the way he did might be a satisfying intellectual explanation, but it does not make living with it, or with him any easier."

"You are probably right. It was hard to live with him, but believe me, it is even harder to put up with this post—mortem guilt. I got it coming and going. I wish I had been a better person."

"You were, Sarah, and very brave on top of it. Consider the case from another point of view. You were lucky. Very lucky. Abused children often turn out to be abusive adults, reenacting the horrors of their childhood. He could have mistreated you and Marisa in a hundred ways."

"Right. I do believe that at some level I knew about his problems all along. It was not rational knowledge, only some sort of intuitive awareness, which told me that the man was damaged, and like a time bomb he could explode any moment. On the one hand I was afraid of him, but I also felt compassion for him, as if I knew that he could not help himself. This vague understanding kept me at his side. Had I not felt it, I would have probably left years ago. It was not by poetic coincidence that I likened my marriage to La Solfatara, long before I knew about his youth. Yes, I guess I am very lucky that the dormant volcano never erupted."

When Sarah was well enough both physically and psychologically, she moved home again and left a void in the big house.

In late February Katharina took her daughter to an island in the Caribbean Sea, where an old friend offered his vacation home and the services of a native live–in couple, who took care of house and garden, and also cooked the meals.

"Your doctors advised against running alone barefoot on the beach," she told Alexa, "They think you are still far too rickety. You have a choice between two chaperones: Gary's mother, or me."

"You call this a choice? I consider it blackmail."

A week later they left the ice– and snowbound city behind for a vacation of indefinite duration.

TWELVE

"I still can can't believe we are doing this," Alexa said as they waited for their luggage at the airport. For some reason a local band was in the arrival hall and very vigorously and with lots of animation offered a rich repertoire of electrifying music; people laughed in response, some moved to the irresistible island rhythm, and started spontaneous conversations with whoever stood next. Everyone was obviously intoxicated with a bubbling holiday mood.

"Doctor's orders," shrugged her mother.

"Yours."

"I'm still qualified. Does it make a difference?"

It really did not. Everybody agreed, family and doctors in perfect harmony, that Alexa needed a long rest to recuperate. Interestingly enough, contrary to general expectations, she did not put up a fight against the plan, but only asked that her mother accompany her.

The sky was overcast when they arrived and the rather long drive in the taxi, and then in the boat, did not offer the picture–book tropical paradise they both expected.

"At least we won't burn in the sun on our first day," Katharina consoled her daughter.

The house at their disposal was simple, but charming and spacious, located in splendid isolation among bougainvillea bushes and fig trees. The terrace, facing the sea, offered a wide scope of vision without exposing to curious eyes those, who sat there. The house and its garden were separated from the seashore by a black wrought iron fence and a gate. There was a large swimming pool in the garden, surrounded rather incongruously by Grecian columns, which reflected in the water. Ana and Pedro, the couple greeting them, appeared comfortable and cozy, like a pair of old slippers, and the punch they served (*nada*, on account of Alexandra) with a tray of delicately herbed lobster puffs, spoke of highly refined tastes in the kitchen.

"So this is how the poor white trash lives! Give me a second to get used to this," laughed Alexa as she kicked off her shoes. It was good to see her laugh again, although there were still dark shadows under her eyes and she was not just slim, but alarmingly skinny. But as the days rolled on, she gained color, a few pounds, and laughed more readily.

On the day after their arrival the weather cleared, and the leisurely routine of the great escape was easily established. They spent the early morning hours on the beach, where they read, fed the gluttonous seagulls, collected way too many seashells, then returned to the house for brunch. Ana was an inventive and gifted cook, and served the most unusual, but tasty meals on the terrace, from where they could see the endless blue of the sea, the palm trees, many of which bent close to ground as if they wanted to lie down in the sand for a siesta. Next to the terrace an overgrown clump of seagrape added a polished deep–red counterpoint to the variation of blue. In such a surrounding the brunch became an aesthetic and sensual experience, which never lost it   initial charm.

"So perfect, so very perfect," sighed Katharina. "Martin too would have loved this place." Alexa was silent. Katharina's constant reference point was her husband. She still seemed to interpret the world through his eyes.

In the afternoon heat they slept, then returned to the beach to indulge in more idleness. In the evening, before supper was served, they took walks, and much later, when the moon rose above the treetops a swim in the pool completed the day.

"How long can one stand doing nothing?" Alexa wondered one evening. The sun was still hesitating on the horizon and was busy painting the water with gold–orange glow.

They were sitting on a bench near the fence in the flower– scented garden, doing nothing more strenuous than waiting for the pre–dinner cocktails to be served; just looking at the moving waves was a very satisfying occupation. Katharina noticed the yellow notepad in Alexa's hand, but made no remark; she saw that Alexa was getting well, and was slipping back into her old habit of making lists, or jotting down ideas. To Katharina this sign of renewed interest was the perfect gift, and the lovely evening enhanced her joy; obviously they had the worst behind them and Alexa would be completely healthy again.

"I have no idea how long we'll find that loafing is fun, but before boredom sets in, we'll take excursions to some of the islands, provided you are willing to tolerate a pair of sandals on your feet for the duration." Alexa nodded, but seemed preoccupied.

"Mom, have you ever wondered why I got ill so suddenly?"

"Yes I have. Doctors have different theories about the cause of ulcers, but stress seems to be an important factor. "

"Yes, I was stressed."

They were quiet for a while, and seemed content with silently enjoying the peaceful early evening.

"Mom, Gary betrayed me," Alexa said suddenly. Her voice was lost in the gentle evening, and the sea splashed and murmured nearby. Katharine whipped around to face her daughter, because she thought she did not hear it right.

"Say it again," she finally responded. But the sorrow on Alexa's face was obvious; there was no mistake. "It is probably nothing but malicious hearsay," she finally said in an attempt to make the ugliness disappear.

"No, it isn't. Gary himself told me."

"Is that why you wrote that e–mail to me before you got ill?"

"No. I had no idea then. Had I known it, my note would have probably sounded more homicidal than frustrated."

"You never said anything!"

"I was trying to find my bearings first, and then I got sick before we could have talked about it."

"My poor darling. Your shock and pain must have been unbearable."

"You said it, Mom. Shock, rage, sorrow, nausea and everything else. I hated him then, and still am not very sure how I feel about him now. This is the reason I was so willing to come here. I wanted to get away, have some distance, lots of it, to see how I will deal with this."

"Was it serious on his part?"

"Heavens, no. She is an insignificant trollop from his company, sort of everyman's Barbie. They attended a conference together in Palm Springs. There was some drinking, fun and games. She was aggressive and available, and very much part of the raging party mood. The only reason she was sent there was to perk up the guys with sensual distractions after endless hours of pointless discussions. Otherwise she is a nobody at the firm. Most likely he would have forgotten the sorry event the next morning, but for some reason she took it into her head to pursue her conquest further, and was (and still is), constantly after him. Or so he says. Anyhow he regretted it almost immediately and also found out quickly enough what an unsupportable stupidity it is to start an affair, no matter how brief, with a coworker. And when said coworker has brains only the size of a pea, and on top of it has nebulous issues of her own, things can really become sticky. Gary then considered asking for a transfer to be away from her. A transfer! Never mind what I want, and never mind if I want him after this –he made his decision and is convinced that all this will leave no mark on our marriage. All we have to do is run away and things will be well again. It is beyond him to even consider that I'm a good hater and just might kill him for this. Naturally he is contrite and believes that saying 'I'm sorry' is like a band–aid, and it will take care of the hurt. His self–assurance and credulity are of heroic proportions. He never considered me, my job, my interests, Laura's school, or my absolute need to be near you. He made a gargantuan mess and decided that to solve it, he must tear up roots, and run. *Après nous le deluge.*"

Katharina took the ice cold hands of her daughter into her own, and sat silently listening to this shocking tale in the gentle night. Out of experience she knew that there is a time in every woman's life when even the most understanding words would act as oil on fire. She understood Alexa's pain, but from the distance of seventy years and after two happy marriages she did not perceive Gary's trivial discretion as a tragic occurrence. This however was not the time to share her opinion with Alexa. Katharina liked Gary like a son she never had, and was going to do everything in her power to help them over this rough spot. But not right now. Katharina's job was to guard Alexa from over–dramatizing the situation, and to prevent her from ultimately sinking into the black hole of martyrdom.

"Darling, give yourself the luxury to grieve and to be royally pissed off. It is part of the healing process. But don't overdo it. You are not widowed, so there is no need to jump into the pyre. Anyhow, it's not done nowadays. Besides think of it, who would be most hurt in the funereal fire?"

Katharina did not possess the easy sorcery of words, which was Alexa's gift. She could not come up with lighthearted salvos, which always caused a smile, depressurized the problem, gave sudden ease and a promise of hope. During the terrible weeks after Martin's death Alexa called her regularly, sometimes even several times a day, and she could bring her mother to laugh at a time, when laughter seemed the most unlikely reaction. After she hung up, Katharina often wondered how she accomplished this psychological trick, but could never understand, let alone imitate it. She wished now that she had that skill to make her daughter see that the world is not about to go under. It was Alexa, who finally broke the silence.

"Some hot shot psychologist once said that married couples are not only soul mates, but also world class anomalies, because they are intimate enemies as well. You go to bed with him, iron his shirts, balance his bank-books, bear his children, cook his meals and then bingo, you want to kill the bastard."

"And go to jail for it? You are not really practical."

"I guess not. Besides, death is too good for him. "

"Homicide is messy, and there is no perfect crime. With your luck a star sleuth like Columbo, Quincy, or Kojak would show up, and discover a tiny piece of chance evidence, which of course escaped everybody's attention. After that, the inevitable follows: off with your head."

"All right, I won't kill him then. Instead, I can picture some choice punishments for him. He could be castrated for example. With a rusty knife."

"By a dilettante."

"Without anesthetics."

Alexa cried then, and her mother put her arms around the shoulders, which apparently could carry the burdens of others so splendidly, but was about to break under her own load.

"Have you talked about this with Gary?"

"Plenty. As a matter of fact, we were quite noisy about it. I could have put a fishwife to shame. The last of our shouting matches occurred the night before I got sick."

"And the results?"

"Other than my ending up unconscious in the ICU, nothing worthwhile. He thinks I'm making a big deal of something that is not worth a hill of chicken shit. He thinks we should forget it and continue living where we left off, preferably in another state. Or perhaps on an other continent. He did not yet suggest that we leave the solar system, but I am expecting the announcement any day soon. But if this woman means nothing to him, if she was no more than a careless fling, a one–night stand, then why flee? What is he afraid of?"

"When you were five years old, you thought I knew everything. Have you not learned since then that I am not the wise woman of your childhood? I don't know the answers. I did not know what to say to Karen when she moved home again, and I am just as helpless now, although I do not see Gary's indiscretion as the grandmother of tragedies. But I am not the one who has to live with him. It was of course stupid of him, but not really evil. It was a mistake and not a crime."

"Mom, I no longer know what is right and wrong. It should be clear, because it was always clear. Now I am lost between the two."

"Give it some time, Love. The fog will lift and you'll see clearly once again." Katharina looked toward the house then stood up."I want our drink now, would you like one too? I'll go in and beat Pedro to it."

"I'd sell Gary for it, but I know your regime and have no hope of getting a real one. I will settle for one without the alcohol. That is the price I have to pay for taking a vacation with a doctor and a mother."

Katharina returned with Pedro, who carried glasses, ice, and two pitchers of a fruity concoction, which Pedro called the "bird". It was made of carefully measured quantities of rum, cream, banana liquor, galliano, pineapple and orange juices over ice. He kept a double supply of it ready in the refrigerator. The one for Alexa was without alcohol; fruit juices and bottled aromas gave the flavor to hers. It was Pedro's contribution to their summer recreation. When Katharina asked him why it was called "bird", he told her that it could make her feel so good that she'd feel ready to fly. Alexa tasted hers, and nodded in approval.

"It is excellent, although I wouldn't mind having the socially correct amount of alcohol in it to make me silly. I hope that after I die I'll be allowed to lounge on a soft cloud with a tall glass of this, while somebody gives me a body massage." Pedro returned to the house to give Ana a helping hand with supper, and silence settled over the garden., while they sipped their drinks. "Let us not talk about Gary any more. This evening is far too beautiful to waste on him. Instead, would you like to know as a doctor and as a mother what I felt before I passed out on that night when my stomach gave up on me? It is a better topic than Gary."

"I would, provided it does not upset you. Tell me all about it."

"I won't tell it, instead you'll read it to me, so I can hear how your voice exorcises the evil memories. I expect to be reassured. After I felt better and was also severely bored in the hospital, and while the impressions were still fresh, I wrote down what happened to me."

The late afternoon was balmy, fragrant and the leaves shimmered green and gold from the departing sun. The moon, pale and insignificant compared to the martial glow of her irresistible and unreachable brother, the sun, was just rising on the opposite side of the horizon. As she rose in the east, he, uncaring and full of himself, was ready to depart in the west, hardly noticing her.

Katharina always thought that the Greeks had it all wrong. Apollo and Selena could not have been siblings. She always felt that his disdainful behavior and her ardent admiration was more like the incompatibility of two magnificent lovers, forever at odds with each other. Theirs was not the usual behavior of brother and sister. At least not in Katharina's romantic fantasy.

The moon now rose a little higher, gaining a bit of brilliance, but it was not her own; it was only the borrowed, magnificent brilliance of the sun that reflected on her barren, cold face. He knew this of course, and with a mixture of contempt and pity looked back fleetingly at his pale devotee, and then disappeared. She knew that it was pointless to chase him, yet never stopped pursuing him. He would never be hers, not even for a single night, yet she could not give him up. At least we had that, Martin and I, Katharina thought. We met and held on to each other through magical nights and brilliant days as long as we could. We didn't fade away with yearning and loneliness rushing in opposite directions. Not while he was here.

The air was loaded with romance and loveliness, and was not made for disclosures about betrayals, marriages in trouble, or the recollection of near death experiences. Or perhaps it was just right so, because its liquid beauty softened the harshness of Alexa's unusual tale, written on the lined, yellow legal pad. She was still too weak to use the laptop when she composed the story of her experience; she could not sit up long enough for that. But her handwriting, even when executed in a half–sitting position in bed, was well–rounded, uniformly controlled and legible. Up to the eight grade she attended a Catholic all–girl school, and the nuns had magic ways to train their students in all the arts they felt were important. Distinguished handwriting was one of them, and Alexa learned well. She handed the legal pad to her mother.

"It isn't very long; you can finish it before dinner is served," and Katharina started to read he daughter's account:

"On that day I came home earlier from work, because I felt absolutely miserable. The argument with Gary the night before still stuck in my throat. I had some awful stomach cramps, which did not surprise me. Every time I am upset, my stomach screams. Gary upset me in a big way, and the pains arrived on schedule. But somehow it was much worse. I was dizzy and weak and had no idea how I arrived at the house, unless my car has a secret homing instinct. I just made it to the bathroom and the pain doubled me over. When I finally threw up, it was all blood. I know that doctors are familiar with blood and it does not frighten them half as much as it does the rest of us poor, common people; to us blood spells pure terror. I was scared and paralyzed and needed help.

"What is the number one has to call in an emergency? 911, or is it 199? Or do I dial the operator? I taught my children this simple fact, as soon as they could walk and talk. They knew all about 911 before they knew how many toes they had. How come that suddenly I could not remember and could not help myself?

"And how does one behave correctly in the event of an emergency? I could write a doctoral thesis about that, and a script for a sit com about the way I flunked that test. It is hard to accept how stupidly I acted.

I was in the master bath when I got sick, and where I sprayed blood and vomit all over everything. The phone in the bedroom is but a few steps away from the bath, and I could have called for help from there. Yet I made myself go all the way downstairs to the kitchen with a bath towel in front of my face, to make the call. And why would I do such a brainless thing? Because I worried that the blood, spurting out like a geyser by then, would not come out of the white carpet in the bedroom! Tiles are easier to clean. To think that I was occupied by such trivia in that circumstance of absolute terror! It makes no sense, but than nothing seemed to make sense just then.

"*The stretch from the bedroom to the kitchen, down the endless steps is a long way when you think you are dying, and by the time I reached the kitchen and the wall phone at the far end of it, I was at the end of my strength. Dizzy and terribly weak, I slid down to the floor, pulling the receiver with me, God knows why. Perhaps in my befuddled state I was hoping that someone could hear me as long as I had the phone in my hand. We were forever talking about exchanging the old phones in the house for that new model, where you dial right on the receiver, but it never came to that. For a second I glanced up to the dials on the wall, and knew that it was way too high, and I lost the strength to pull myself up to punch in the three numbers.*

"*I then looked at the dangling phone and panicked. To think that the difference between life and death was only a question of a few feet of wire dangling vertically just above my head! Or the unaccountable procrastination about exchanging the phones for a newer model! If Gary would not have arrived when he did, the light would have certainly gone out for me. I was retching blood again, was choking on it, and my head weighed a million pounds, and I needed a pillow. I think I pulled the little chair under my head thinking that it was the pillow I needed.*

"*I'll try to write exactly as I experienced it, which is not easy, because after I collapsed in the kitchen, my mind did not seem to function the way it functioned close to half a century. I was confused and kept drifting in and out of a gray world, which was neither consciousness, nor the lack of it...*

So there I am on the floor. For a while I am surprised to see myself spread between the planning center and the wine rack, and I am aware that I lost a shoe and that the skirt of my suit has slid up. I am also aware of a lot of blood, but do not know where it came from, or how I got there. Was someone pushing me there, or did Gary send me to sleep in the kitchen, because he has a mistress and wants me out of the way? My back is cold and some sort of strange electricity flashes through me, which in turn diminishes my body, then again makes it expand almost beyond endurance, to the point of explosion. My muscles let go, then again they contract cramp–like; my face is hot; my eyes are burning, but I can't open them. Or maybe they are open, only I can't see a thing. I'm hurting all over, and somebody is tearing my stomach from my body. I'm shivering, because great sheets of ice cover me, and somebody keeps pulling me down into deep water, while others are pushing my head under. I am terrified, because I cannot get any air and am mortally terrified of being alone and even more terrified to go under. The water closes out all sound, but the waves hitting something, perhaps the walls, are echoing and thundering in my head. I can't remember why our kitchen is under water. I always wanted a swimming pool, but why did he put it in the kitchen? Where was I to cook if the kitchen is under water? Or maybe he does not want me to cook any more. Ever again. I am superfluous. Other women are younger and more beautiful; Gary can choose from a wide selection. He already has. I am getting old and have to live under water from now on. But I cannot go on living with this pain. And soon all my blood will be gone.

"There was once a goldfish that died. When I fished it out of the tank, it was no longer red, but golden pale. Did it too lose its blood? And the waves keep hitting the wall and I hear it from an ever increasing distance. I am lost on a gray and endless body of water. How could this happen to me, and why didn't Gary tell me about converting the kitchen into a swimming pool? And why was it important for somebody to pull me under? Was it his mistress trying to kill me? The pillow is hard under my head and there are pink, purple and gold stars falling out of my mouth, and out of my fingertip. The pillow is hard, or is it really a pillow? Perhaps it is not. It is the executioner's block. I am perhaps Mary, Queen of Scots, waiting for the sword. Or Marie Antoinette, waiting for the blade of the guillotine to fall. I won't mind losing my head, but the block under it is really hard. My last minutes on earth are painful and uncomfortable. Rocks keep falling into the ocean. But that doesn't make sense. I must wake up. Ice is falling into waters. Into oceans. The ice that falls into the ocean is called something, But I do not remember what. I cannot remember anything. It is called something starting with the letter g. Goosenecks? No that is either part of a lamp or part of a bird. I don't like either. Goosestep? That too is something bad. And the ice sheets, with the starting letter of 'g', are all falling on me, and soon I will freeze and die if somebody does not cover me. I must keep on thinking, because if I stop, then it means that death has caught me, and I don't want to die. Do I first freeze and then die, or is it the other way around? My skin is hot and then cold, and finally it is quite dead. My inside is turning into red—hot bubbles and the bubbles join the stars and I burp stars and bubbles and evil things. Or is it blood, which is coming like a torrent from my mouth? And is the blood good or bad? My inside is falling apart, rotting away, the cells and atoms going crazy. What caused it? I do not understand, but I must keep thinking in order to stay alive, in order to get help. Somebody has to pull me out of the water and stop this deadly spinning down, down into a bottomless pit. Somebody ought to punch in the magic number that gets me some help. I feel a little better now. The pain has eased and I feel relaxed and very light. I no longer care about falling into another universe, and do not feel the cold so much either. I can think a bit clearer and even remember that the ice sheets are called glaciers. I suddenly recall the Möbius strip. I was introduced to it by a wonderful teacher, but I forgot her name.

The strip was very impressive, and still is. I twist a ribbon and paste the two ends together. Then take a pencil and move it along the middle of the strip, and find that a miraculous, continuous line can be traced without crossing an edge. The strip has one surface and one edge. I start somewhere with my pencil, anywhere, and suddenly I'm on the other side, on the backside of the strip, yet, I never lifted the pencil and never crossed over an edge. Fascinating. From one universe right into the next, from one dimension into another. And I never even noticed when I crossed the line. Is this then death? Crossing over without being aware of an edge, any edge, and finding myself surprisingly on the other side of a topography, in a different universe? And then the realization: I'm fading and nobody here to help. The few lucid moments I had are getting muddled again.

"But my pain and my fear no longer bother me. My body feels slack, I am terribly weak, but my mind is still working. Not clearly to be sure, but rather in a jumbled manner. It still spins out fragmented memories, and I remember a few tasks I must do tonight, before Gary comes home. I am not sure what these are, but it will surely come to me after I feel a little better. But somehow nothing makes sense and nothing is important. I can hardly keep up the effort of keeping my mind going. I want to go to sleep.

"But then, the relief of perfect inertia is interrupted. Somebody, or something is pulling my body out of the water, and I wince. Why can't they leave me alone when finally all pain is gone and I am starting to feel good? They didn't come when I needed them, why fuss now, when finally I am well on my own? Something pricks my arm and a new, strange element is forcing its way into my bloodstream and I cannot resist it, or scream against this outrage. Against my will somebody is introducing a foreign element into my body. I am violated, and this thing that enters me, makes me powerless and meekly obedient. Evil ghosts come with rough, searching hands over my body. They force my mouth open and push horrible things down my throat and I cannot protest or scream. I am at their mercy. There is a forest, or perhaps it is not even trees I see, but only legs. My mind clears a bit and I'm wondering about the difference between a forest of legs and a forest of tree trunks.

"A long forgotten memory comes swimming into my confused mind. I am little and we are late for church. Mom stops with me in the back of the church, I alone among adults, mostly men. All I see is their legs, standing around me like barren tree trunks in shades of black, navy and gray. It is very scary and I feel that soon I shall suffocate. Now these malevolent trees are back, but most are white. The ice and snow, which chills me to the bones, covers them too. The dark trees of yesteryear turned white with ice. I am helpless on the floor among the snow covered trunks, and I know that they'll get me. They know the time

has come when they find no resistance. They stand around me, forming a fence from which there is no escape.

"Suddenly there is a piercing pain in my throat. The executioner is cutting my throat as a punishment for a crime I did not commit. Where is the judge to whom I could appeal? I am alone, so alone, and so scared. Gary is not here, because he has a mistress. My children are lost and my mother is at the cemetery visiting Martin. No one here to defend me. These evil things can have their pleasure with me. There is a mad rushing sound around me, like so many crazed birds circling, hitting, humming and swooshing. The birds pull me from the floor clucking with nasty joy because they are finally getting their victim. They place me on a rolling, hard platform and tie my helpless body carefully to it. I can't escape or defend myself. Then they push my cot with supersonic speed into a great void, which is surely the end of everything. I close my eyes and decide to complete my dying in order to escape the ghosts, the birds, the tree trunks, and the final crash. I don't remember the rest."

Katharina put the legal pad on the bench and took her daughter into her arms.

"What a tale of horror!"

"Isn't it? And it keeps coming back to me ever since. I keep experiencing again and again, that hapless condition when I hung witless between the states of conscious and unconscious awareness, and was mortally afraid and confused, no longer in control. I hoped that your reading it to me would exorcise the evil."

They sat quietly, soothed by the night fragrances and the sound of the waves moving with ageless rhythm. After the long day it turned dark, quite suddenly, as it usually happens close to the equator. Overhead passed the moon, dispensing her borrowed brilliance over the dark expanse, which was the sea, and the stars shimmered on the velvet sky like so many jewels on a magnificent evening gown. The garden, lit with elegant restraint, displayed the shimmering vegetation here and there.

Katharina sipped her drink thoughtfully and was haunted again by an old concern: just how conscious is a supposedly unconscious patient? Her patients have been children, and if they were lucky and survived their catastrophic illnesses, they could not tell afterwards what happened to them during the critical time. She often discussed her concern with colleagues, but the answers were vague, often contradictory. Most likely some patients never perceive what is going on while frantic efforts are put into motion to save the feeble life; some mercifully forget it all. But apparently there are others, like Alexa, who are aware of what is going on, even if the experience is frighteningly surrealistic, mixed up with memories, fantasy and fears.

At any rate, later they remember at least part of it, and the fear remains as a residual anxiety.

She remembered how often she told parents to talk to an unconscious child, because it can hear and recognize the voice of parents, and the security of it can help the child to get well. It would be then logical to assume that some patients also perceive the communications or happenings around them during a life–threatening situation, which might frighten them. The perceived ministrations with their inherent terrors could add to the already grave trauma. Perhaps it would make sense to explain each step of the emergency procedures to the patient, exactly as if she were wide awake. Perhaps there are unexplored psychological powers, which could be used while working on the body. She did not know. If such methods existed, the news of it did not reach her. Was I a professional fossil, she wondered. Was I limited to the small field I called my specialty, not really paying attention to what happened in other fields?

As evening took over, Pedro lit the rest of the garden lights. China clinking on glass underscored the deeper sound of silverware being placed on the table, exciting fragrances mingled with the scent of flowers, and it all subtly announced that dinner was about ready and Ana was setting the table. They walked quietly toward the house for their evening meal. On that evening neither felt like going back out for their now habitual midnight swim. Yet, Katharina could not sleep much.

She tossed in her bed for a long time. She recalled the dark circles around Alexa's eyes, her pain–ravaged face, and was afraid the time for hope and forgiving has not yet come. Alexa's unhappiness crushed her, yet it was clear that she must be the lifesaver for her daughter until she surfaces from the misery on her own. The hours dragged slowly, but finally she knew that morning is near. She left her wrinkled bed and walked to the window to wait for the relief the day would bring.

Gray–green ocean waves rolled in, almost unseen yet. The mass of water was still without light; it shivered somber and uninviting in the misty dawn. But soon a burning band would appear at the eastern horizon and the sun would make its spectacular entrance, to create the daily miracle, which never even makes the headlines in the morning paper. She listened to the sounds of the awakening garden, and waited for the happy surging of energy she usually felt at the beginning of a new day. Slowly the veil of night dissolved, and then evaporated, the walls turned lighter.

The new day would bring hope, the most stubborn of mankind's virtues. And who knows? If the day can renew itself predictably and reassuringly, why couldn't a worn, slightly tattered relationship do the same?

Ana was already busy with the tasks, which made life so pleasant. The tantalizing fragrance of strong coffee, touched with a hint of cinnamon and brewed to perfection was coupled with the equally exciting fragrance of freshly baked croissants. Picking up her robe she walked out to the terrace to commune with the new day, and to indulge in the sensual pleasure of Ana's breakfast. As the sun poured over the terrace it seemed inevitable that Alexandra would get well again and that somehow her problems would resolve themselves.

THIRTEEN

The heat was oppressive and even the constant breeze from the sea did not bring relief. The world was waiting for something. The water, coming at the beach with bands of restless white foam was strange, alien and aggressive, and carried bits of troubled flotsam. Seaweed, bits of wood and broken shells were scattered on the sands of the beach.

"This is no fun today, and the undertow, which I hardly noticed up to now, is frightening," Katharina finally announced. "Let's go back up to the house and the safety of the pool. "

"Some big weather is brewing up," Pedro said as they arrived at the villa. "Even if the radio had not just announced that a storm is moving in, I would have known. Old bones foretell the weather better than those meteorologists. Also listen how quiet everything is. The birds are still, and the air has a funny color. Ana started to move things into the house. If you won't mind, we'll serve lunch indoors today."

"Not at all. The sea is rough and we won't go back down. As a matter of fact, we'll leave for a few days this afternoon. I heard that the mountain on the east side of the island is easy to climb and we'll try it."

"It only pretends to be a mountain," Pedro said with contempt. "It is barely a hill."

"So much the better. We are hardly experienced alpinists. I made reservations for a few days in a hotel up there; I would like you to organize a cab for us, if you'd be so kind."

"I can do that easily, because my brother is a cabdriver, and would be glad to take you. But are you sure that you want to go on a tour, when an incoming storm is announced?"

"If a storm comes, God only knows which way lies safety."

The weather was unusually still, the heat suffocating. The taxi had no air-conditioning, and by the time they reached the point at which modern transportation had to give up, Katharina had second thoughts about the wisdom of the outing. If the cab would have been any cooler, she would have returned home before embarking on the rest of the trip. As it was, they got out of the cab at the crossroad marked by a shrine, a bar, and a souvenir store. Katharina paid the fare and directed Pedro's brother to make a detour on his way home to drop their two bags at the hotel, where she made the reservation.

They stood for a while looking after the departing car and Alexa sighed,"Now I know how the sailors must have felt when they watched Hernando Cortez burn the ships. There goes our means of escape. We are stuck, Mom."

"You are so dramatic! For one thing, we could reach the beach from here one way or another. Pedro's brother doesn't have the only cab on the island. Second, after we walked around up there to our heart's content, the hotel, only a walking distance from here is expecting us with a swimming pool, Jacuzzi, massages, 600 thread count sheets, great food, and butler service."

"How do you know?"

"I asked, of course. And you'll love it."

"If you say so."

Walking on a moderately steep and narrow path they soon arrived at a simple column, which marked the highest point of the island. It was really just a flat grassy plateau, and high only in relation to its surrounding. Rough boulders, like toys of an overgrown and bored god–child, were strewn all over. Their elongated afternoon shadows marked strange patters on the dry grass, and the silence was complete. Far below the sea glimmered peacefully, and the great distances disappeared in a blue diaphanous mist. It was worth climbing up to see the wide vistas, even if their cardiovascular system groaned from the insult of unaccustomed exercise.

After a short rest they walked on, skirting the odd boulders, some taller than a person. Alexa was ahead, and was the first to see the shallow pond, not much more than a puddle.

"Come slowly," she cautioned her mother and pointed to the still water. A shimmering, jewel–cloud of dragonflies hovered above the small pond, executing graceful acrobatic feats in the still air.

"Like delicate helicopters, with those slender bodies and gleaming wings!" Alexa whispered. "They are more beautiful than butterflies! So much beauty and all of it is hidden up here, where hardly anybody can see them."

"I am more curious about how much *they* see of us, and how the world looks to them. They have compound eyes, composed of a thousand individual tiny cameras. The insect thus can see up, down, sideways, all at once. But what a vision! To the bug's unusual eyes the world must appear as a composition of minuscule mosaics."

"It would be a nightmare for us, but obviously, the experience is not damaging their *Lebenslust* at all." Alexa said, but smiled at her mother, who once again could not resist teaching. She was born to do that.

"I think I can almost imagine how it must be for the bug," Katharina said. "In October, before he was taken ill, Martin gathered a lot of twigs and leaves in the garden, but it was too windy to start the fire until after darkness has set in, and the air quieted. I was sitting in the study just opposite those lead glass windowpanes, writing a letter, when Martin started the fire. I looked up from my letter, and for a moment my heart stood still from the sight. There were dozens of fires blazing in our garden, right under the window. It took a moment until I realized that the countless beveled glass sections of the lead glass multiplied and enlarged the light of the one modest fire he was tending. It was so unbelievable that even after my brain figured out what I saw, I had to get up and open the glass pane to make certain that indeed there was only one fire. I sometimes think that is how the dragonfly sees our world. " She was silent for a moment as she remembered the remark Susan made just recently. It had no trace of accusation or rancor; it was just a quiet observation of a woman, who understood pain and losses. Odd, Susan was saying, that every little incident brings Martin to your mind. She was right.

It was right, but not odd. He was her life and they were so completely intertwined in each other, and gathered so many rich experiences during the ten years they spent together that it would have been surprising if the whole world around her would not be a vibrant reminder of him. She sighed and added, "The fires were extraordinarily beautiful."

Alexa was completely absorbed in the unusual display of the plenary convention of dragonflies. Without disturbing the performance of the insects, she turned to her mother. "Don't we all see the world in fragmented parts only?"

"If we do, it is different from what these guys see. We see only selected parts. They see the whole thing. True, it is all broken up, but still complete, no part is missing, no part escapes them. This is the enormous difference between their perception and ours."

"I guess you are right. And you are probably right, in as much as you allude to my messy situation, which you probably do. But at this point I cannot be philosophical about it. And I can only see one part, which makes me raving mad. I am no dragonfly."

They sat down on a nearby boulder and Alexa watched the shimmering movements of so many blue and green wings. Katharina was more absorbed in the mood of her daughter than in the charming sight. It was a relief to see her become so interested in something else beside her disappointment and deep pain. Her words spoke of pain, but her eyes followed the shimmering flight of the insects and a hesitant smile brightened her face. Her mother believed the smile, and not the words. The decision to come to the island was paying off, and this excursion today proved how a change of scenery can help get over a hurt.

The air was very still, but the earlier brilliance of the sky disappeared, and a heavy haze, almost like fog, settled over the island. The sea retreated into the distance and changed its color first to a milky gray, then to pewter. The stillness was depressing, the sense of being cut off from the world was no longer exhilarating.

"Let's descend to the hotel," Katharina said. "I am not familiar with the meteorological conditions here, but I feel like a cat when it senses rain."

In less than twenty minutes walk they arrived at the hotel. It was built for people, who were seeking a sanctuary from the turmoil of the beaches; a carefully designed place, where the guests could enrich the soul and indulge the body, and where money was not a problem.

The entrance at the end of a palm–lined alley was impressive, and as they entered the sandstone lobby with its floor to ceiling windows and elegant furnishing, Alexa, brushed her unruly locks back from her face and whispered to her mother, "This does not look like the place where guests arrive slightly sweaty and on foot. If we don't watch, they'll direct us to the service entrance."

But she was wrong. The supermodel, who apparently moonlighted as a receptionist, greeted them by name, and a bellhop was instantly at their side to escort them to their suite. Social position and money permit extravagance and nobody showed surprise at guests, who did not appear in chauffeur driven noble cars.

"We shower, and then I beat you to the pool," Katharina announced and disappeared into the bathroom.

Alexa stepped out to the balcony and watched the meandering waterway flow under bridges, around flowerbeds, spilling into reflective pools, and then continue its way making islands of clusters of palms. The subtle design caused it to disappear and reappear again; its route was capricious and delightfully surprising. Surrounded by majestic palm trees the turquoise pool glittered as the sunlight hit its surface. The stately trees were protected from the winds of the sea, and probably tended by horticulturists, who talked to plants, which explained their perfection. As far as she could see the garden was tranquil, well ordered and basked in the luxury of an unhurried cadence; time was of no consequence here. Those who sought refuge here had no pressing appointments, and lacked the compulsion to return to the fast lane. It was truly a little bit of Eden and had everything, except the sea and perhaps the biblical snake. But after long days of blue and green waters, sandy beaches, and the constant sound of waves, the stillness of the garden, the manmade verdant perfection was relaxing.

"Had I known that life can be this pleasant, I would have gotten sick sooner," she said to her mother a while later at the pool

"Wasn't it an exceptionally good idea to come here for a temporary change of scenery?"

"Mom, all your ideas are exceptionally good. This is a bit off from my earlier vision of simplicity and the desire of walking barefoot on the beach. I also know that it is sinfully expensive."

"There is no sense in hoarding money. As they say, there are no pockets on the shroud; you can't take it with you. I don't propose to throw it all to the winds, but when something is important, one should not hesitate to spend lavishly."

"And this is important?"

Katharina sat up in her lounge and looked at her daughter solemnly.

"Alexandra Maria, know this: nothing, but absolutely nothing is more important to me than your health and well being. I would stop at nothing to help you get strong again."

"You already gave me your blood," Alexa teased, but she was touched.

"I can't help it if you wasted yours, right on the kitchen floor."

"So very careless of me."

Katharina closed her eyes again and rested for a while. Perhaps she slept, perhaps she was just deeply relaxed and did not even notice when Alexa left to slip into the pool. She swam elegantly like a dolphin, barely making a ripple; her multicolored bathing suit was like an exotic flower floating in the crystal clear water. She was getting well again, and seemed content. Strangely she never spoke of her marital problems again, but did not seem as depressed or in such a deep anguish as she was in the beginning. It was difficult to guess what went on in that proud head of hers.

A slight wind arose and it skipped and hopped across the flower beds, but barely ruffled the blossoms. The sky was an opaque greenish color and the stillness almost depressing, nothing moved. Katharina, now fully awake, walked to the edge of the pool.

"Did you come to gather me?" Alexa called from the water.

"Indeed. If I don't, you might just dissolve like a bar of soap."

While waiting for her daughter, she again looked at the broiling sky, so in contrast with the suffocating stillness of the earth. Great black clouds whirled above, intermingling with moving, changing wispier, gray masses.

Sunset

The clouds turned and twisted, sometimes showing a yellowish, sick tint in the center, which covered the pale yellow orb of the sun. The valley turned dark and cold. Then again the dark curtain opened unexpectedly and the colorless sun, short on light and warmth, was exposed for brief moments. A woman of undetermined age with heavy make–up, diamond earrings and a pearl necklace was rapidly gathering her beach things nearby.

"Do you feel it too?" she asked Katharina. "My skin is crawling and I never have been so tense before."

"Pardon, feel what?"

"Why, the coming of the bad weather. The young ones talk about nothing else because it is so exciting, the older ones complain about it, because weather changes are so painful in the joints, and the personnel is exceedingly nervous."

"Indeed, the air does feel different," Katharina admitted, "But this is not the season for hurricanes."

"There is always a first time, and since they are naming them as if they were women, it is to be expected that they would be capricious and do their own thing." With that, she turned and disappeared around the bend. The pool was almost empty by now and workers appeared from nowhere and were rolling the chairs and loungers into a shed, disguised as a small pleasure palace.

"Found a new friend?" Alexa asked as she emerged from the pool. "By the looks of her, she must be a chance refugee from the local cemetery."

"Speak with respect of old age in my presence," Katharina warned. "The calamity of aging is inescapable, and I don't want to be reminded of it. Not when it is pounding ever nearer to me with powerful and frightening steps, only heard in the Jurassic Park."

"Mom, when it comes to age, you usually exaggerate. But what is going on? Where are all the people? And where is all the garden furniture? Are they closing shop? I have gotten used to our midnight swim back at the villa, and resent this early closing time. So terribly low class, don't you think?"

"The woman, you were pleased to call my new friend, said something about bad weather coming up. Pedro said the same, before we left. The natives know what is what. Let's listen to their wisdom and go inside. Anyhow, it's not only getting cooler, but it is also time to get ready for dinner. Make yourself irresistibly beautiful for tonight's candlelit affair, even though you'll have to be satisfied with me as your date."

Alexa did her best, and she was stunning. She combed back her dark hair smoothly, and then piled the rich tresses at the nape of her neck, showing off a perfect Grecian profile. The strapless gown, the color of green sea foam and about as light, was formfitting and simple in the classical tradition. From décolleté to hemline, all around her body spiraled a wide band, embroidered with green and silver beads, sequins and stones. The whimsical gown emphasized her slimness, and surrounded her with a faint glitter of subdued elegance. Katharina looked at her and as so often before, she caught her breath at so much loveliness.

"Mother, you are staring," Alexa teased. "Is my slip hanging out?"

"Haven't noticed. But I see that the tongues of several macho types do hang out."

"Good. I like that. Nothing bolsters my morale better than appreciation without personal demands." She handed her mother a small box, before she sat down. "A gift for you. While you were getting ready I explored the hotel and found this in the gift shop. I thought it too perfect and too appropriate to leave it there."

Katharina peeled away the wrapping paper. In the box, on the white velvet rested a pin in the form of a dragonfly, artfully crafted of amethyst and silver.

"Beautiful! Thank you so much. It perfectly captures, and will hold for ever, the mood of this wonderful afternoon," she responded.

"I hoped it would."

They were finishing the dessert, when Katharina ventured to touch the subject they both avoided since Alexandra's confession.

"I'm in flux and in doubts about Gary," she answered. "I'm still angry and hurting, and castration is still an option, but I now might grant him anesthesia. Unfortunately, I do love the bastard, and although I wonder if I'll ever be able to forget what he did, the initial rage is gone. A little while ago I thought that any day soon I would be canonized, but I was mistaken. My soul is far from pure and it totally lacks holiness or heroism. I don't want him out of my life, but I can't figure out how to let him back in without losing my dignity, or my tattered saintliness."

"Can't, or won't? You haven't asked for advice, but I'm giving it to you anyhow. Don't dwell on the past too much. Turn away from it. Remember Lot's wife." Absentmindedly she refolded her napkin and with an understanding and with an understanding smile waited for the inevitable argument.

"I do, and all the fuss about her looking back infuriates me. She was a sensitive woman and needed a closure. She was not complaining, was not about to run back, or abandon her family. She just wanted to say farewell, have a last look at what has been; after all, it was a significant part of her life. She was a true woman and knew that one cannot start something new by negating the past. I too would have looked back. Sinful, or not, the city was her home and in it were her friends and her memories. No doubt she must have been grateful for the chance of getting away from that particular holocaust, but what is wrong with a final goodbye? I'll try not to dwell on my personal injury too long – but I can't yet step over it. Not yet. I must look back, even at the risk of turning into a pillar of salt."

"I guess you are right. But still, it would be better to leave grudges and pain behind, and not think about them. God and her husband only tried to protect Lot's wife from the agony of seeing the horror."

"And by doing it, patronized her to the point of turning her into a pillar of salt! Some loving help she got! I don't think I can buy that. I can live without such protection. Don't you see? She was gravely insulted in a condescending and witless way. And who knows for sure what happened? She might have been turning into a pillar of salt not because of what she saw, but because she was thoroughly shocked at being treated as a witless semi–animal. When will men credit women with brains and with the ability to conduct life without masculine signposts?"

Katharina was about to answer, when a waiter stepped to their table. "Excuse the interruption please, but severe storm warnings were just announced. We are asking our guests to go to the lower level lounge, and feel comfortable there; the bar will be open. There are built–in, electrically operated shutters on all the windows, which will now be lowered on all openings to prevent injuries in the eventuality of shattering glass. Please, don't be alarmed; the management is only taking the precaution for your safety. The nightlights in your rooms will remain unaffected in any event, and there are also candles and flashlights in case the electricity would go out. Despite the weather condition, we'll try to make your stay safe and pleasant." He glided to the next table to repeat he instruction.

Silently and efficiently the shutters, deceptively light as if they were nothing more than Venetian blinds, rolled down simultaneously, and instantly closed out the frightening world. Inside the lights burned brightly, the air–conditioning hummed, and the guests felt safely enclosed in the architectural cocoon.

But through the walls and the shuttered windows the wind could be felt. Not yet heard, but somehow felt. It slipped through the manmade safety, and touched the nerves of the glittering, coiffed, gowned and pampered guests. And the guests shivered as they felt the power of something they could not see, understand, or control. Conversation halted, then surged into excitement, then again it diminished into primeval fear, just like what the caveman experienced when he first felt the rage of the winds.

The waiters were fluttering among the tables, discreetly holding their flashlights which were not yet needed, obviously eager to usher the guests into the lower level of the building. But the guests were still procrastinating; nobody wanted to be the first to go, and be labeled as one who is afraid. For some people, appearances are important even a split second before total destruction.

But then the wind lost patience and meant business with a sound very much like the thundering of an oncoming train. It started somewhere in the distance and everyone knew what it was. Suddenly nobody needed the urging of the waiters, and obediently the shimmering wave of evening gowns, accentuated by the dark suits of the men, moved downstairs with surprising speed. Nervously laughing and feigning bravado, they joked on the way down, and tried not to listen to the elemental fury, which had the power of ripping off roofs, tossing around cars, shredding power lines and whipping up the sea.

"I just heard about the weather on the radio, before I came down to the dining room" a gentleman said. "We are not really getting the brunt of it; its path is supposedly near the shoreline."

"You are an angel, or a witch," Alexa said quietly to her mother. "Whatever suggested to you to choose this particular day to come up here? It is bad enough here, but can you imagine how it is down there at the villa?"

"Yes I can. I hope Ana and Pedro are all right. Perhaps they have experience in how to survive this. As soon as it blows over, we'll call them."

As if to contradict her intentions, the lights flickered, and then went out. Some screamed, others laughed in the sudden total darkness, but the waiters were already lighting the candles and carrying trays with glasses of champagne and cocktails.

A middle–aged man of obvious authority raised his voice and asked for attention. He introduced himself as the manager, and informed the guests that the hotel has its own generator, and even as he is speaking it will take over the servicing of the hotel's cooling system, refrigeration, kitchen appliances, the lighting of the stairwells and hallways, and the filtering of the pool.

"What you will experience is a brown–out," he joked. "You'll see some lights, but not nearly the brilliance you would expect. We have no idea how big the damage to the power lines is. It might be repaired in a few hours, or a few days, or a week; therefore, we are going to be frugal with our self–generated electricity in order to preserve the food in the freezers and refrigerators, and to put hot meals on the table for you. We'll only turn on the air–conditioning for short periods, mostly during the time while meals are served. The phone lines are gone, and it will be some time before we know the full extent of the damage done by the wind. Please, bear with us, and thank you for your understanding and cooperation."

A musical ensemble, unnoticed during the first excitement, emerged from the shadowy background and started to play discreetly in a vain hope to drown the screaming of the wind.

"Didn't they play music on the deck while the Titanic was sinking?" a bejeweled matron asked. Her companion took out a cigarette from his gold etui, and waited for the waiter to light it. He inhaled deeply and with pleasure, then turned to her and said in a light tone, "I don't see the connection."

"They traveled in an unsinkable contraption, designed by experts, and had no real fear until the very end. Music seemed appropriate to them at the time," she explained. "Realization came too late."

"Are you indicating that we too are staying in an indestructible contraption, built by experts? But it is not the same. We do not have an icy ocean under us, our building is not broken in two, and they just lowered the storm—proof shutters a while ago," he argued.

"That is just it. I have lost faith in experts, and discovered that man—made things are rather fragile, and they are habitually and easily destroyed either by Man, or by Nature."

"You are a fine one with your doomsday picture! We have a storm, and it is a bad one, but it will soon blow over, and life will go on as before."

Champagne was offered to them and they changed the topic.

"At least I am not the only one, who would rather be somewhere else," remarked Katharina.

But conversation gradually resumed, although obviously everyone only made a show if it. Ears were all tuned to the outside and followed the raging of the storm as the sound of it filtered in through the safe walls.

And it did make itself be heard. It thundered, and hissed, rattled the indestructible shutters, and angrily smashed objects around. The screaming of the wild winds was punctuated with dull thuds, and the conversation in the lounge would stop a few minutes, while the guests tried to guess what was destroyed.

But eventually the storm moved on. As a precaution, the shutters were not raised and the guests had no idea about the degree of destruction. Butlers guided the guests on the dimly lit hallways to their apartments, and most of them found that despite the excitement, sleep came easily.

FOURTEEN

Katharina and Alexandra slept late in their darkened, silent bedrooms. Apparently everybody else did too, because no noise filtered in to disturb their late sleep.

"Did we dream the storm, or did it really happen?" Alexa asked midmorning after emerging from the bath. Her mother, dressed and efficient as ever, already called room service for tea. The blinds in the living room were raised, and the sunlight pouring into the room was so bright that Alexa shielded her eyes from the invasive brilliance.

"If it was a dream, then it qualifies as a regular nightmare. After you have put yourself together, we'll go down for breakfast and for news. Did you rest well?"

"I'll tell you as soon as this tea does its magic."

The breakfast room was cheerful; a shimmering day greeted the guests, as if the storm did not happen at all. The topic of conversation was naturally the storm. Telephone and electricity lines were still down, but news filtered in through cell phones and portable radios, and were also described in the daily newspaper printed in the hotel and placed on the breakfast tables.

The hotel and its surrounding area were not damaged much, and the debris swept by the wind into the compound was already cleaned away by the hotel crew. The auxiliary generator did its work perfectly; the breakfast room was cool, the coffee hot, and the perfect pancakes were served with sizzling bacon strips.

The news was all about the damage along the shoreline, and about the still impassable roads, blocked by debris, fallen trees and electrical wires. Although the storm was less vicious than feared, and did not even qualify as a hurricane as predicted, true to the imperative of common tropical storms, it did destroy enough. The airports small and medium, on all the islands were overwhelmed by tourists, who wanted to leave, especially those, whose hotels or vacation homes were as damaged as their holiday mood.

Pedro and Ana had no cell phones, but after several futile attempts Katharina was able to reach a neighbor, who had one, and whose number she luckily had. He gave detailed report about the damage, said that Pedro and his wife were safe, but advised the women to stay at the hotel for a few days, and enjoy the luxuries which are temporarily not available at the villa.

"Enforced leisure was suggested," she announced to her daughter after the phone call. "Some of our roof is damaged, and the electricity is still out, which means no hot water, no hot food, no cold drinks. The sea is still angry, or at least irritated, and the swimming pool, with its filter at a standstill, is probably full of stuff you don't want as bathing companions. Might as well enjoy our stay up here."

Katharina and Alexa were not big eaters, but the extravagantly loaded Sunday buffet table was a temptation not easily ignored.

"The obvious cosmic injustice has proven its existence once more," Alexa remarked.

"Why so?"

"Don't you see? The privileged are less vulnerable even in natural catastrophes," she answered as she contemplated the buffet tables.

Katharina did not respond. She was not prepared for a discourse on social inequities, and was unashamedly happy that her daughter, despite her concerns, was showing more interest in food than before. Mothers have priorities, even after a great tropical storm, even if in other circumstances they are as sensitive as Katharina. With their plates filled, they returned to the table.

"I am not sure about the truth of it, but I seem to recall reading somewhere that the Chinese, when meeting friends, instead of asking 'How are you?' greet each other with 'Have you eaten?'" Katharina remarked, as she shook out her napkin. She was trying to atone for her social insensitivity displayed a minute ago.

"How strange!"

"Not really. Consider that when the answer is 'Thank you, I have eaten well,' it means that you are wealthy and healthy enough to buy and to eat food. In that context the exchange makes excellent sense."

"Yes, perhaps it does, especially from the point of view of a nation, where hunger was, and perhaps still is, a way of life, and a bowl of rice the ultimate gourmet ecstasy." Alexa spread the butter on a roll, but before she took a bite, she said quietly, "The truth of this becomes especially clear after a demonic illness, when you are convinced that you'll never eat again, never would enjoy the luxury of food. Only then can you realize that the simple act of eating is a gift we seldom appreciate, because it is to natural." She took a small bite of the roll, and then said more cheerfully, – "For a long time, even after I was well again, I pictured this ghastly scar in my stomach, and imagined that any kind of food swallowed would irritate it. But it hasn't. Doesn't. I hardly think of my insides any more. Hail to modern medicine!"

After brunch they walked out to the pool, just like most of the guests, who sat up camp at various spots in the semi shade. The women were made up as for the opening of the theater season, were clad in designer swimsuits, and adorned with cascades of jewelry usually kept in the vaults of bank safes. They were magnificent, like exotic birds at the height of mating season, except they were totally ignored by the males, who played bridge, studied the financial pages, or dozed. Katharina and Alexa read. Sleepy peace settled all around the pool, which lasted until teatime.

Later, when the heat of the day was tamed by the incoming sea breezes, it was Alexa's idea to walk up to the high point, where they saw the dragonflies. "I just want to see if they survived the storm."

Taking their time, stopping often to look down into the valley, and at the endless sea reaching to the far horizon, then dissolving in the blue haze, they arrived at their destination. The little puddle was much larger after the rain, and the dragonflies were just as active performing their aerial dances. They must have found a good hiding place during the rage of the storm.

But the two women were not alone. Sitting on a rock and gazing intently at the shimmering insects was a man. His lean body was clad in white slacks, a flowing white shirt, and he wore white walking shoes. He was neither old, nor young; there was an aura of agelessness about him.

The two women stopped hesitatingly.

"Good afternoon, ladies," he said, and there was a gentle smile in his eyes and in his voice. "I hope I am not disturbing you. I often come here on weekends, and have never met anyone before."

"We don't own this place," Katharina said pleasantly, "Also, we were the ones intruding."

"Well, since I also don't own it, we could perhaps peacefully share it, and watch the sun go down. Seeing it from this point it is quite a spectacle. It is also a nice get–away from the incessant rehashing of the storm." He gestured with his hands at the surrounding boulders, as if he were receiving distinguished visitors and offering them chairs in his palace. Choosing rocks with flattened tops they settled down, unconsciously upholding the illusion of guests taking their seats.

Although he looked ascetic, there was also sweetness, wholeness and even worldliness about him. Katharina, who usually respected the privacy of others and never initiated conversations with strangers, had the sudden desire to talk to this man, who appeared calm, almost spiritual.

"This is such a charming place. Do you often come here?" she asked.

"Just on the weekends. I work the rest of the days and that does not make such outings possible."

"I am surprised, because I imagined that you would not have a common life with a humdrum job like the rest of mankind," she said in a bantering tone, but immediately regretted the intimate tone she used.

"But I do have one, most assuredly." His voice was deep and pleasant and he spoke with a slight British accent, which she found pleasing. He looked at her with serene interest and his clear eyes sparkled; his look penetrated beyond the mask of her face, beyond the cells of her body, and appeared to enter into her very soul. Yet, his searching, probing gaze was neither uncomfortable nor invasive; it expressed not curiosity, but human interest and an expression of love seldom seen among humans. Only Martin could look into her eyes with the same deep caring and empathy. "I do work, and my job, measured by most standards, is rather mundane. Humdrum? I don't know about that. I rather like doing it."

"I used to love to work," Katharina said.

"Yes, I imagine you did," he assented, and his smile was a benediction. Suddenly Katharina wanted to have the approval of this strange, mysterious man, but she blushed instantly at the childish notion. "I can't imagine life without work, nor could I do work which I don't like," he continued. "Work, done with love is really just another form of worship. It is the kind of prayer that does not ask for anything, but just is for its own sake. Don't you think so too?

"I have a friend, who believes that activity helps resolve difficulties."

"I agree. Idleness negates life, and it also removes a person from the stream, which moves toward a grand purpose."

"A purpose?"

"Not a man–made one, to be sure, but one that was carefully designed for mankind." Katharina bent down, found a stick, and drew circles in the sand. Personal reluctance kept her from spilling her soul to a total stranger, and so preferred silence.

"Very unusual," she finally murmured.

"Not so unusual, only we are mostly disinclined to talk about it." Silently she agreed to that too. After a while he continued to talk unperturbed. "It also helps to achieve the wholeness, which is part of our goal on earth."

"I read about that somewhere."

"Then you know that we need to do certain things to be spiritually and physically healthy and alive. Meditation, work, laughter, thinking, emotional involvements, relaxation, fun and games, even eating and drinking, are part of it. That is what I mean by wholeness, and it is also part of the grand purpose."

She did not answer. What he said was indeed no great news to her, but coming from him at that time, and in that tone the statement was invested with deeper meaning. Dressed leisurely but elegantly, flashing an expensive wristwatch, he sat comfortably on the hard rock and radiated the patience, the wisdom, and the endless serenity of Asia. He was not just charismatic, but appeared to have a magnificent secret, something that could make life once again a joyous knowledge, a burst of happiness. It was simply good to be with him; he had a positive emanation, which had a calming effect upon her. It has been so long since she felt so very good and content, and so very safe.

"Once we realize that we need to strive for this sort of wholeness, we know that we cannot pigeonhole our interests," he continued slowly, obviously weighing carefully what he said. "The way I see it, we can't confine ourselves exclusively to intelligent cogitations, or deeply emotional experiences, or to the living and material world, nor to work, or to religion alone. We need to integrate it all, and give equal care and intensity to each. Isolation into any one of these categories may cause the soul to wither, or else fuel insanity. The only exceptions to this rule are the born geniuses, or saints but for the rest of the common mortals the unity of spirit with body is essential. And so work, willingly and with love performed, does have its sacred place in the order of things."

They sat silently for a while and it occurred to Katharina that when Jesus was teaching the multitudes, they might have been sitting just as quietly after one of his parables, thinking about what the words meant, letting the message sink in. She was sure of the great silences when the masses congregated to learn from the master–teacher.

"So we strive for wholeness and harmony." It was not a question.

"Can't do anything else; it is so ordained. We are all minute sparks, broken off for an infinitely small time, really just for a flash, from that splendid brilliance, to which we all belong, and to which we'll soon return. The fracture of a millisecond, which we spend on earth loses its entire significance as soon as we return to the magnificence from whence we came." It was of course Alexa, who had to argue:

"Once upon a time, Lady Violet Asquith, immersed in a deep philo-sophical gloom, remarked to my all–time hero, Sir Winston Churchill, that in terms of infinity we are no more than just cosmic dust, just worms. To which the irrepressible Sir Winston answered, 'Perhaps, but I am a glowworm.' I feel the same way. Don't minimize my existence."

"I admire your heroic optimism, and the self–assurance you share with Sir Winston Churchill," he laughed.

"You talk about life after death with remarkable assurance," remarked Katharina cautiously."It is one of those things we all wish to believe , but find it very difficult to accept. If afterlife is a condition where we forget all that went before, it ceases to make sense to me. On the other hand, if in an afterlife we still perceive things of the mortal world, than it must be a state of unmitigated agony, rather than happiness." He shrugged at this.

"Do you recall the death of Alcides? I guess in your country he is better known as Hercules. His father was Jupiter, and his mother a mortal woman. Jupiter consoled the grieving gods at the funeral pile of Hercules, by telling them not to despair, for only the mother's mortal share perishes in the flames. The other part of Hercules came from Jupiter; therefore, it is divine and immortal. Johann Schiller described in a poem called 'Ideal and Life' how the godly part was taken from the flames and how it soared upward into celestial brightness, into joyous and unwonted lightness. I imagine something similar. We'll lose the mortal part for sure, but the other part, the divine, which is also very much part of us, will continue to live and be content and exquisitely happy. Poetry and religion after all, are not all that far apart, are they?"

For a while the silence was unbroken, but then Alexa asked him, how he came to know these things about existence, life purpose, and the immortality of the soul.

"I am not sure that I know anything," he answered lightly. "I don't consider this wisdom. I think it is common knowledge." Again there was a brief pause and then he continued with ease. "Anyhow, how do we get knowledge, common or otherwise? I am not sure. We listen to others, we read what others wrote, we observe and think, and then integrate it all. Suddenly we feel that what we know is self– evident. But of course, the thing gets a bit muddled, because we no longer know what was our very own thought to begin with, and what was something we distilled from the thoughts of others. But ultimately it does not matter, does it? We are what we are. We are as whole and as complete as is humanly possible to be, and it does not matter where the building blocks came from."

"Therefore, I am not even myself, but merely the sum of thoughts and feelings of others, the result of countless influences gathered on the way?"

"It is my belief that it is so. Isn't that something?"

"I really don't think so. It sounds like plagiarism on the grand scale," Alexa answered but with less conviction than before. Katharina knew that her daughter was fiercely independent, and that she worshipped the individualism of man. She expected nothing less than more argument from her, but it did not escape her that Alexa was gradually mellowing.

"Not at all," he answered patiently. "We get knowledge, inspiration, and spiritual fuel from others, but we don't steal anything. It simply falls on us, like sunlight, which warms and tans us, or like the air, which envelops and sustains our life through the oxygen it carries. This knowledge prevents us from becoming soulless humanoids, who are motivated only by love of pleasure, fear of pain and death, and by a huge and wretched hunger for fleeting things." His words hung in the air and Katharina wondered who this unusual man might be. A philosopher? Teacher or psychologist? A religious thinker or writer? A mystic? What sort of a person speaks so freely and easily with total strangers? But he continued to talk in his leisurely manner. "And then remember, we don't take all this without payment, because we too add to the emotional or intellectual storehouse of others. Just as we are enriched , so we enrich others. Mankind is a great living entity, an unusual symbiotic community. We all benefit from each other, and are all part of that great universal magnificence some call the Prime Mover, or God, from where we came from and to where we shall return. Unfortunately, we can also be equally destructive to each other," he added.

"It sounds like man doesn't have its own mind!" Alexa argued.

"Far from it. No matter how we rely on each other, we still keep our uniqueness, because we all inherited different genes, and absorb different ideas, which we interpret differently. You and I might see the same play, or hear the same music, but it is unlikely that it would affect us exactly in the same way, because, we are also wonderfully individual. Do I ever really know what sort of shade do you perceive when we both contemplate something that is commonly called 'red'? Do we really see the same color? Do I experience your pain exactly as you do? Hardly. No two of us are exactly alike. This makes the system so very beautiful. Also, while we have this communal dependence necessary for our growth, we are not left alone to find our way haphazardly; we have someone with us at all times to guide us." He was absolutely serious, yet seemed to be amused and even happy as he reflected at some unspoken thought. His attitude seemed somewhat contradictory: the sophisticated and intellectual approach was colored with an almost childlike belief in wonders; yet, this contradiction did not appear out of place and was not disturbing. His clear blue eyes were gazing at the world with the innocence and seriousness of a very young child, yet a passing thought would suddenly illuminate his face, and a smile just as innocent, but infinitely delightful would change the contemplative look into one of boundless joy. Suddenly he and his surrounding appeared to be in a flood of sunshine.

Alexa glanced at Katharina sideways, but the calm face of her mother did not show any surprise, or even a shadow of a sneer at this fantastic announcement. The conversation was heading into the esoteric, and Alexa was never comfortable with that line of thought.

A gentle wind, no more than the sigh of the departing day, came up from the valley. The passing day painted the hills, the trees, and rocks with an ever deepening shade of blue; soon it would be time to turn back to the hotel, away from this strange encounter and back to the safe luxury of the conventional. This extraordinary meeting on the hilltop was bewildering; the territory they entered was alien, and she almost wished for the superficial chatter of the guests, which at other times irritated her.

"Some would interpret this by saying that a guardian angel guides us," he continued unperturbed. "Others, of a more rational breed, cannot picture an asexual Somebody, with great white wings watching their steps. They find it downright offensive," he smiled as if he too only half believed this. "But nevertheless, there is someone, a force, a power; something, which is uniquely ours, and can appear whenever we concentrate on it and wish its presence. At times it is called conscience, or life force, or the instinct for survival, an extraordinary sixth sense, whatever. But it is there. We all have it, there is no doubt about this."

"Wouldn't it be wonderful, to have such a companion!" Alexa said wistfully, in spite of her rational reservations. "What would be more perfect than to have such an all-knowing being to lean on, someone who could suggest what to do, and how to deal with life's underhanded blows."

"But you do have one!" he insisted. "Everyone has one, no matter what names were given to them in different cultures. This spirit is with you all the time. He cries when you are sad, and laughs when you are happy. He drinks from your wine and sits at your bedside when sleeplessness and sickness torment you. He is yours, and yours alone. He has no other care in the universe, except you. Your job is to find the way to communicate with him."

"It is a beautiful idea, but far out, light years beyond the limits of reality," Alexa argued. She could not buy into such an idea. He looked at her with kindness, and apparently was not offended by her incredulity.

"Have you never felt, especially when you were alone, a sudden heightened perception, a deeper consciousness, a spiritual unfolding?" he asked. "At such a moment you are far above matter and above the raging seas. Your spirit flies high and free, whispering dreams to you, and you have the sense of revelations, which come from outside of your own, regular sphere. You are full of riches; limitations disappear. New ideas enter your mind and you are able to suddenly see how to resolve a problem. These suggestions, or vibrations if you prefer a modern word for it, came not of this world, yet they are imminent and useful, because they whisper to you the right decision, the right road to take. Despite the exalted feeling, reality is keenly present. Your self expands and your soul feels measureless and deep. You feel good and powerful and suddenly you see the right way."

"Put it this way, yes, I felt that way sometimes. But only for very short moments, and I was clueless why it happened, or what to do with it."

"You have to work at it. You have to practice calling this force and when it comes, you have to train yourself to hear it and to understand its message. It gives you the power you need. Meditation is the way to achieve this."

"Power! I think the world needs less rather than more of it. Power is so evil," Katharina said. She considered this stranger to be some sort of a guru, sent their way to answer questions, and to thaw them from the winter of their grief. It did not appear odd to her that she would ask such deeply personal questions, nor did it surprise her that she was willing to accept his answers.

"Power, when guiltless and responsible, and when used properly, is nothing but constructive energy, without which no action is possible. Only self–serving power is destructive. But I must not impose on you any longer," he added rising. "At times I have the tendency to hold forth like a self–anointed preacher, the kind I deeply detest, and do not wish to be like. It was a pleasure to talk to you. Who does not enjoy a captive audience?" he added with a chuckle. " However, decades ago I learned two important things: you have to get up from the table before you are satiated, and you must shut up before you become an insufferable bore."

Standing he appeared even taller, and as he prepared to say his farewell, he was undeniably the perfect gentleman of the world. There was a quiet deference in his attitude, and his expression conveyed that the encounter was pleasurable to him, and the parting regrettable. Katharina remained seated, hoping that her reluctance to say a formal farewell would keep this man a little longer in their company. He looked at her again with that gentle, penetrating look, but said nothing. His power over her was beyond understanding. It had nothing to do with attraction between sexes, nor with instant friendship. He was a force, a source of light, something she never experienced before, and was reluctant to let the sensation go. She was still puzzling about that unusual magnetism he had, when Alexa offered her hand to him.

"The pleasure was ours," she said simply.

He held her hand a little longer than customary and after a short silence said, "I do not know very much about the female psyche, but I feel that you are deeply hurt. I also suspect that when women suffer, it usually has to do with the loss of love."

Alexa nodded silently to affirm his remark and looked toward the puddle, but the dragonflies were all gone. Evening was approaching and these insects knew well enough when to leave. For a fleeting moment she marveled, how he knew about her problem, and also how he dared to talk about this most private affair, but she was not truly offended. He was more like a doctor, who probed the sick places before he prescribed the medication. She would not think of hiding her symptoms from a doctor, nor from this superhuman man, who just might have the cure for her soul.

"Love can truly crucify you, because it is not always the harmonious pleasure it is cracked up to be," he said in a tone that made the last of her irritation disappear. "Love is experienced as an ecstatic condition only in the very beginning of an affair. But true love transcends the great passions as well as personal desires and then it comforts, supports and forgives. Or at least so I heard, and so I read."

"And you think that this general renouncement of personal desires would compensate for lost hopes, and would lastingly satisfy?"

"Don't ask me, because I am not an authority on that, or on anything else. Women, the more enduring and the more sensitive of the species, know the definition, its extent, and also the pain of it. Ask a wise woman for an answer. But I do know one thing: love cannot be a confining, suffocating prison. To be able to grow in love, each of the partners needs space; it is not possible to develop in each other's shadows. And," he added with a chuckle, "according to some biologists and sex experts, monogamy is the most deviant behavior in nature. When it is found, it is almost headline news." Alexa could not answer. This man had the capability to look into the deepest corners of her soul, and spell out her problem, and this was becoming increasingly more uncomfortable, frightening. Who was he?

"Yes, I too read Olivia Judson, but for heaven's sake, she is talking about bugs and fish, and not about creatures with immortal souls," Katharina, taking Alexa's side, argued. She noticed the sudden silence of her daughter, and recognized that this probing caused pain. This stranger knew too much about them. Without planning to do so, they permitted him to glance into their most private thoughts and emotions, which were really none of his business.

"Oh, but how do you know what sort of souls those creatures of water, land and air possess?" he asked, but laughed heartily to take the edge off his remark. He too noticed the sudden withdrawal of his companions.

"Perhaps female bugs and fish don't mind their partner's philandering, but women of the human species are more demanding in their relationships than your average field–cricket lady," Alexa's voice was again cool as she spoke, and her irritation flashed warning signs. She noticed too late that unwittingly she gave away what troubled her. That was the last thing she wanted to do.

"I told you that I am not an expert. Losses and disappointments are inevitable, even necessary, but remember, you can forgive, and you can choose either joy or pain. I assure you that it is quite possible to find the golden mean between sinful self-immolation and impossibly exalted integrity."

"It is easy to say, but hard to do."

"Very true. But than nobody in this Universe promised us that life would be easy. Look, the sun is setting," he added turning to the west, and then back to Katharina. He looked into her eyes for a dizzyingly long moment, then completed the thought: "Day is gone, work is done, the sun dips below the horizon; it is time to leave."

"If you are alluding to the passage of time and of life, exclude me from the grand scheme," Katharina said half–seriously in an altered mood, while trying to reestablished the distance she preferred with a stranger. "This eloquent closing prayer does not apply to me. My day isn't done, my work isn't completed, and I'm not leaving yet."

"Good, I'm glad to hear it," he shrugged playfully, and even added a slight, polite bow to show his agreement."However, the sun will set on schedule, as it always does." Surprisingly, he made her feel good all over again.

They shook hands, the man smiled, and the smile wiped away the last of the angelic attributes from his face. He looked very human and very charming in the way only men of the civilized human race can be. He bowed with old–fashioned elegance and walked away with light steps. He most certainly did not have white wings attached to his graceful back.

Long after he disappeared around the bend, the two women still sat on the rock and thought about the words just spoken. Despite the discomfort of letting him a bit too close to forbidden territory, and of using a tone too familiar between strangers, the two women felt an emotional vacuum, a sense of being forsaken after he left. His unusual talk left a deep impression and they both wished him back. Finally and regretfully they started their walk back to the hotel.

FIFTEEN

Mother and daughter were silent in a companionable way, each pursuing private thoughts. Values and goals had to be reoriented. Pain had to be sent away somewhere. The problem of tomorrow had to be faced. Decisions had to be made. Like men during the gold rush they too sifted through an amazing heap of sediments to find the nuggets worth keeping.

"Don't laugh Mom, but there was something ethereal about him. I mean, he was the closest thing to an angel. It was a religious experience." Alexa said breaking the silence. "Or am I cracking up? I did hear talk like his before, but it came from a pulpit on a Sunday morning. To tell the truth those speeches didn't half as much impress me as the sermon of this stranger."

"What a sad comment on our advanced civilization! If a man rises above common superficialities, we consider him otherworldly." Katharina smiled as she said this, but there was a tired, sad echo in her voice.

"He was unusual, even though some of his ideas, like the one about the guardian angel, was a bit extravagant. He also read us like open books, and somehow it surprised me that he talked so matter–of–factly about philandering," Alexa summarized.

"He was fascinating. And intelligent. But unlike you, I liked his guardian angel theory the best. I wish I could make him, or it, appear whenever I need him," Katharina admitted.

"Which do you mean, Mom? The stranger, or the guardian angel? Both have a lot of appeal, but the flesh and blood version was extremely handsome, and refined to a fault. I wonder if under all that polish he too is the kind, who would leave his dirty underwear all over the place, or if he would raid the fridge after I cleaned up the kitchen creating instant mess. Not likely. He is too spiritual to eat, or to have dirty underwear. He probably does not snore either, and respects the tiles in the bathroom. And hopefully he does not engage in extramarital flings."

"Leave our friend alone. True, I found his invasive X–ray eyes somewhat disturbing, but he was not that far off from what people have believed long before Christianity was established. Ages before modern wisdom drove out old beliefs and with it the use of our sixth sense, people used to believe in personal spirits."

"If you say so, Mom. I suppose you have enough data to prove your theory." Alexa guessed what was coming. Katharina believed that all she had learned through the years, must be handed down to her daughter.

"I certainly do. Most Catholics believe in guardian angels, or in saints, who can help resolve their difficult affairs."

"Really?"

"Really. But before them the Romans also believed that every man had a benevolent spirit assigned to him at birth to protect him through life. Men had their Genius and women their Juno, and thus equipped they could face life bravely. The Romans honored them and offered sacrifices at their altars. And even before the Romans, people always believed that there were good, or evil spirits to influence their lives. That was at a time in the evolution of humanity, when the two hemispheres of the brain were perhaps not as markedly specialized as they are now. Today external realities are processed in a twofold way: the left side analyzes and categorizes, the right side, the territory of the Muses and of angles, opens new vistas and wraps the experiences in powerful magic. Way back in the beginning , when the less rigid separation of the spheres let impressions flow back and forth freely, information then was interpreted in a less specialized and perhaps richer way. Add to it superstition, usually born of general ignorance, and you have the picture. Intuition, 'gut–feeling', 'seeing with the mind's eye', talking to angels, and making leaps of insight were not outlandish, but just another way of knowing things. Or perhaps our ancestors were just more gullible. We'll never know for sure. This was a time, when people heard miraculous voices, had revelations, 'second sights', and perceived things, which are hidden from us now. Miracles happened then, as they are probably happening now, but in those less complicated times, people were able to see them."

"Mom, do you realize how frighteningly left–brained you are just now? You can't help but examine and explain things, can you? You really missed your vocation," Alexandra laughed, although she was well accustomed to her mother's apparent need to explain things. This was so since Alexandra could remember, and she supposed that it would never change. She looked at her mother with deep affection, and posed the question in a bantering tone, "Are you indicating that many generations ago we would have perceived the appearance of this man as a messenger of the gods?"

"Very likely. But in the intervening years we lost the faculty of awe, and are much poorer for it. We now have the tendency to work through our experiences with the analytical left side, and ridicule or at least dismiss as fantasy anything unusual. We are pleased to categorize men as eccentric, because instead of trivial chatting they share their philosophy with an audience. Our friend at the beginning of the twenty–first century is no longer a vision, only a clerk on a weekend stroll, who prefers to talk about spiritual things instead of baseball, weather, money, or politics, and that of course, is unusual enough. But the significant difference is that this meeting did not make us rush back to the hotel to urge the Sybaritic guests to leave their pre–dinner cocktails, and their pleasant superficialities. We would not think of asking them to come up here to the site of the "vision" to fall on their knees and pray. Nor are we moved to erect a temple or a church, or at least an altar where we met him. Our ancestors would have done that, you know. Our perceptions changed. The encounter will be totally forgotten, unless you are willing to bring some flower sacrifice tomorrow to the site. At best, we'll make amusing table conversation of our encounter, but more likely we won't mention it to anyone, lest we make the impression that we are too eccentric to be trusted."

"And that would be social suicide, wouldn't it?" Alexandra teased. Her mother understood the intent, but she only shrugged.

"Personally, social exclusion means little to me. It is clear though, that through gradual evolution we are ever more rational and permit the left side of our brain to be overly dominant. On the other hand, our angelic friend found a way to revive the forgotten talent. He discovered the skill of how to activate the other side, which is believed to be more creative and insightful, and so he learned to commune with his inner self. Apparently, he can recall his Genius at will. I actually envy him for it."

"Mom, don't outanalyze him from our life! The man was beautiful; he was a gift. I would not go so far to say that he was a miracle, but he most certainly made this evening memorable. I rather liked his gentle way of telling us about benign spirits in whom I don't really believe, yet wish it were so. I would like to have an angel, whose only job in the world is to take care of me, and who would walk even now with us, and would help make a decision about Gary."

"I thought our gentleman–angel told you clearly enough what to do about Gary and about love."

"I got that. But it was easy to feel that way while his saintly and suggestive presence made all mundane things trivial."

His ideas, eminently sensible, were easier to accept in theory than in practice. Alexa saw clearly enough that she could either run, or she could forgive. She could examine the hurt, the disloyalty and dwell on it in perfect agony. Or she could be done with it forever. Turn the page, start a new capital. There were no other choices. The difficulty was that she could not really choose either option. Not yet.

She also understood that to ask someone to forgive a sin is terribly difficult, but not nearly as difficult as to forgive a transgression. It is easier to hang on martyr–like to the wounded self, and perversely enjoy the pain, which is steadily growing out of proportion. One can create the illusion of a morally elevated status at the expense of the sinner. The worse the transgression, the more noble the self, while enduring it. To forgive might be divine, but what is left to comfort the injured soul after the absolving?

This was a proposition too tempting to ignore, even for noble–minded Alexandra, who was usually above the pettiness of self–aggrandizement; yet, she was not totally immune to it. Latent yearnings for heroism, martyrdom, or anything to lift the person above the crude insult is too beautiful and too satisfying to miss. It is a compensation of a sort. One can truly be glorified while suffering eloquently from the wrong–doing of others. To forgive and to forget would rob the suffering victim of the meager satisfaction of feeling superior.

"The 'angel' made me understand that I could be disgustingly moral, provided I forgive Gary. And strangely, I was just about ready to do that," Alexandra said, "But the glow is all gone now. My good intentions and noble sanctity went down the hill with him."

"Don't let the saintliness rub off you so rapidly," Katharina mocked, and then added. "Try to get over your hurt. You don't want to leave Gary, because you still love him. Don't play up a silly incident to look like a Greek drama, or even worse: like a soap opera. Forget, forgive, and grow. Consider that through compassion and understanding you could find the old peace and contentment. Not all at once, but one step at a time. Darling, you do have a marvelous thing; don't let it slip out of your hands because of false pride, or spite, or because of a silly dime–a–dozen woman of no consequence."

Alexandra did not answer. She agreed with her mother, but admitting it would be a first step of forgiveness. She did not yet feel strong enough for that step. Katharina seemed to understand her daughter's inner turmoil and changed the subject. Alexa had to work out the solution on her own.

"I liked what he said about work," she said in a light, conversational tone. "He was so right about that. Never before did I consider idleness immoral, but he is right. It is. When we get back, I'll call City Hospital. It is a teaching hospital, and Ed is telling me they are forever beating the bushes to find teachers. I could do that. As a matter of fact, I want to do that. I have the required love for it."

"And expertise."

"That too."

The sun was gone, but it left a glowing rainbow–colored sky behind, which slowly faded to pearly iridescence. The wild path widened, rocks and visions were left behind; here the road was paved. White flowers collected the last of the day's light and shimmered in the gathering dusk, brightening the undergrowth. The bare trunks of tall palm trees, living and majestic columns, marked the way back to the hotel, back to the familiar, the safely conventional. The flower– scented air felt light and beguiling.

Katharina inhaled deeply; the loveliness of the evening was almost unbearable. She looked ahead out of the dark tunnel formed by the vegetation overhead, and beheld the last of the purple and gold light the departing day splashed on the western horizon. This is it, she thought with exploding joy and boundless amazement at an inspiration, coming totally unexpected from somewhere, she knew not whence. Why could she not see this before? She had to close her eyes for a moment to arrest the vision and when she opened them again, tears of joy clouded the sunset. The twilight hid the uncontrolled emotion, but Katharina was beyond caring about appearances, or about preserving dignity; she was elated.

She knew without doubt that the thought, coming as a sudden revelation, was not just a gossamer fantasy, but was as real as life itself: one day Martin would appear at the end of some road, perhaps similar to this one. He would be clothed in light and beauty, waiting for her patiently in the relaxed pose she knew and loved so well. Fine wrinkles around his eyes would appear as he smiled and asked her in a voice, once again warm and strong, what took her so long to meet him. He would take her arm and guide her out of the dark tunnel into the magnificent brilliance, and into a new and different state of consciousness, so unfathomable and splendid that she could not even start to imagine it with her earthbound mind. In this new dimension temporal and material considerations would not exist, and the self would merge into perfect love and expand with absolute knowledge.

Through an entire life consciously, or fumbling blindly, the spirit was always striving and thirsting for this conclusion, and on reaching it, the bliss, the ultimate gift of the Creator, would sanctify the soul, and make it worthy to unite with the Universal Soul. The soul, her soul, would instantly recognize the formerly elusive, eternally magnificent ecstasy, which was promised all along, never fully believed, but nevertheless freely given. Finally with exquisite triumph certainty would take the place of mean doubts and of hopeless fears.

It would happen exactly so, and yes, Martin would be there, waiting to guide her into this unbelievable experience. For a moment they'd stop and he'd put his arms around her, and kiss away the hollowness of the lonely years when he was not at her side, and then they would continue their flight into eternity.

Yes, this is how it'll happen, she repeated the promise silently. It was such a luminous, never–before–felt sensation that for a moment she felt faint from the sheer grandeur of it. Her heart expanded with exquisite joy, it lifted her above the material world, and the horizon stretched into endless vistas. She fully understood the silent revelation, and unquestionably believed it; and yes, she was looking forward to it. Otherwise, how could she go on living?

A pale moon appeared, ringed with a milky halo, and a million cicadas sang their evening prayers. She walked on lightly, happily, cherishing the secret promise in her heart. This was as definite and matter–of–fact as anything she ever experienced in her long life. This was a promise she could count on.

They were almost at the hotel, when Alexa unwittingly broke the magic of the moment as she talked once more about the unusual encounter. "He mentioned meditation. We could actually try it, don't you think, Mom? At least it does not have any side effects like so many medications do."

Katharina looked sideways at her daughter to see how serious she was, but had no time to answer. Alexa stopped in her tracks and stared ahead at a man approaching, dressed in khaki pants and a light summer shirt. Despite the deepening dusk and decreased visibility, she was certain.

"Gary!" she called. After a second of hesitation he moved toward them, and then Alexa was in his arms.

"When I heard about the storm, I could not get through to you per phone," he said holding her tight, his voice muffled by the richness of her hair. "I sold my soul for a seat on an airplane, and offered my future for standing room on the boat. I had to be sure that you are unharmed." There was a short pause, and then he asked in a very low voice, "Will you forgive me and come home with me? Please!"

Strong, self–assured Alexa cried in his arms and told him, "Yes. Yes!" And then regaining her habitual light tone, added with a short , throaty laugh, "As long as you don't expect me to move to the Andromeda constellation, or to North Dakota." And I promise that I won't choose this ghastly pain, this self–mortification and senseless condemnation any more, to all of which I'm getting dangerously attached, she wanted to add, but decided to keep the thought for herself. Too many words could ruin the magic.

"Andromeda? I don't understand, which is not unusual," he said still holding her, "But that doesn't keep me from loving you. If you can forgive and forget, we could start all over. We had so much..." His voice was wistful, and she knew what would matter to her from now on.

They walked silently the rest of the way.

Was this stupid and inconsequential event in her daughter's married life necessary? What did it mean and was there a lesson in it? Katharina did not know. Her mind, trained to look for cause and effect searched for an answer, but she did it only halfheartedly. There was so much more to life than just rationality.

The new security of a promised future, of a mystical transfer into a different world made her strong. She could now accept with a measure of tranquility what life on earth offered, which are tribulations and triumphs; plenty of pain and joy; errors, mistakes, losses and new beginnings. It is indeed a difficult thing, this life on earth: strangely beautiful and awful at the same time. But it is all so precious, because after all, this is the only life we have in this particular dimension.

Her grief, or Alexa's anguish were nothing out of the ordinary; everybody has his rich share of troubles. Some thirty–two hundred years ago Achilles, by nature not really a pessimist, already discovered (at least Homer says so) that there are two sorrows for every blessing. Nobody walks through life unscathed and even the most fortunate ones will eventually have to face their own mortality, which is an overpowering event, regardless whether the man lived as a saint or a sinner. Ultimately he is measured by how well and how bravely he mastered the ups and downs between the two ends of the continuum, between birth and death.

What was the meaning of losing Martin? She did not know, but since the new assurance that he is not totally gone and is waiting for her in some form, in some dimension, in timeless time, she felt warm, peaceful and protected. Tomorrow may come as scheduled. She no longer felt disjointed, nor abandoned, because she knew that at the end of the road something indescribably happy and complete awaited her, a graceful, blessed ending to a good life.

The End

Sunset

COMMENTS OF READERS ABOUT PREVIOUS BOOKS

<u>This Old House by the Lake</u> (autobiographical):

"The gifts and defects of age have always fascinated me. This gripping story of rebuilding and building a house, life, a relationship and a loving restingplace, at a mature age, in the little–written–about society of contemporary Hungary, in a village little changed since medieval times, was a page–turner for me. It is one of those books, which makes you like people more – all the people in the book, even the most tardy and inefficient workman. It is infused with the plucky, anxious, wonderfully–open–to–happiness personality of its heroine, the writer, and has a strong, silent hero in her husband. A pro–life book, in every sense."

Nuala O'Faolain, author of bestseller books
ARE YOU SOMEBODY? and MY DREAM OF YOU"

"…had me laughing and crying. It is a real personal story of trial and triumph, and at its most important level, it is a story of love—the kind of love for which we all hope. In an earlier age the author's husband might have found a place in Carlyle's 'Heroes and Hero Worship'. An enriching experience in reading."

Dr. Andrew Stangel, art–historian

<u>The Countess and her Daughter</u>
(Was awarded a Gold Medal)

"A many layered story, unbelievably sensitive and expressive. The author seems to know what love, the most elusive fantasy, is all about. Her violin has six, instead of four strings."

Max Leonard, school principal

Beyond Conventions

"…delicate and captivating. The story sweeps across two centuries and the reader is compelled to keep the fingers crossed for the protagonists to find their way out of the restrictive social mores of a bygone era.

Dr. F. M. Duffy, historian

The author was an educator and administrator in the US Department of Defense Dependents Schools (DODDS) in Germany, where she taught classes for the gifted children. After working a few years as school administrator, early retirement followed. She and her husband now live in Ohio and in Hungary, where they converted a "disaster area" into a lovely home (described in THIS OLD HOUSE BY THE LAKE), and spend their time writing and practicing what they have been dreaming about.

ISBN 141209148-9